Midnight...

It seemed like a dream that she, an American girl, should be walking at midnight with a boy through the streets of a village that once had been a Roman fortress, or that her father should be held prisoner in the great hulking castle that loomed before them in the light of the moon.

"If something goes wrong..." Megan's heart was pounding, for András' hands were on her shoulders and his face was close to hers.

"Nothing will go wrong," he whispered. "I promise you...if I may kiss you."

GOOD-BYE TO BUDAPEST

Jeannette Eyerly

JEANNETTE EYERLY

GOOD-BYE TO BUDAPEST

BERKLEY BOOKS, NEW YORK

This Berkley book contains the complete
text of the original hardcover edition.
It has been completely reset in a type face
designed for easy reading, and was printed
from new film.

GOOD-BYE TO BUDAPEST

A Berkley Book / published by arrangement with
J. B. Lippincott Company

PRINTING HISTORY
Lippincott edition published 1974
Berkley Highland edition / January 1976
Berkley edition / July 1980

ISBN: 0-425-04523-4

A BERKLEY BOOK® TM 757,375
Berkley Books are published by Berkley Publishing Corporation,
200 Madison Avenue, New York, New York 10016.
PRINTED IN THE UNITED STATES OF AMERICA

For Marilyn

Contents

1 THE BOY IN THE BROWN RAINCOAT   1

2 THE MEETING AT THE METROPOLE   13

3 INTRODUCING DR. DOZSÁS   29

4 A VIEW FROM THE HILLS OF BUDA   43

5 BLACKOUT   61

6 "SUCH A PRETTY LITTLE OPAL"   73

7 THE OTHER NATASHA   89

8 ALL ON A SUMMER'S DAY   105

9 THE CASTLE OF THE KINGS   125

10 GOOD-BYE TO BUDAPEST   139

   EPILOGUE   149

1
The Boy in
The Brown Raincoat

THE BOARDING AREA was crowded at the Frankfurt airport where Megan More waited for her flight to Budapest. She didn't mind. If the direct flight from London to the Hungarian capital had not been canceled, she would not have been in Frankfurt at all. And if she had not been looking everywhere, taking everything in, she would never have seen the boy in the brown raincoat. But unless she was mistaken, there he was! The same boy she and Kate Cade had seen only that morning in London!

Just as they had come out of the Cades' apartment on Piccadilly, across from the dazzling greenness of Green Park, Kate had grabbed her arm and pointed a quarter of a block away. "Look! It's him!"

"It's *he*," said Kate's mother. Although the words had been spoken almost as a reflex, Kate

1

picked them up and continued without taking a fresh breath.

"It's he. The boy we saw yesterday when we were getting your visa."

"I know," said Megan, who not only had seen him before Kate had—her eyes were very keen—but was looking at him so intently she did not realize that Mrs. Cade had flagged down a taxi until it pulled in to the curb and she heard her friend's mother say, "Heathrow Airport, please."

While the driver stowed Megan's luggage into the front seat, the girls continued to stand on the sidewalk staring at the corner where the boy still waited.

"Look!" Kate cried needlessly. "A taxi is stopping for him, too! Where do you suppose he lives? Where do you suppose he's going?"

"Girls, *please*." Mrs. Cade spoke with resignation from inside the taxi. "I hope you realize that precious time is passing while you two stand there acting like a couple of teenagers."

"Mother and her humor," said Kate, not unkindly, and followed Megan into the cab.

That conversation had taken place hours ago. Now, alone in Frankfurt, Megan shifted her overloaded purse from one shoulder to the other and moved around a stout woman with a bulging string bag in each hand who had managed to obstruct her view.

She had, however, made no mistake about the boy. He was standing near the door through which she herself, having cleared security, had passed but a short time before. He was wearing the same brown raincoat he'd worn in London, the cinched-in belt too long because of the narrowness of his waist, the same black beret pulled down over the dark curling hair that was, in length, just right. Today a rolled-up newspaper—it looked like *The London Times*—protruded from the pocket of his raincoat. The day before when she and Kate had been on their way to the travel agency to get her Hungarian visa, he'd been buying a copy of *Newsweek* at a newsstand near Piccadilly Circus.

Even on a gray day with a mist of rain falling and a mass of people swirling about on the sidewalk, he had stood out. They'd passed by him almost close enough to touch, then had gone on to the Breedlove Travel Agency on New Bond Street just two doors away. When they emerged almost a half hour later the sun had come out. And the boy was still there, standing with his back against a building reading his magazine.

Stating the obvious—it was her only, or her *almost* only, irritating trait—Kate whispered that he must be waiting for someone and Megan, of course, had agreed. At any rate, it had given them another chance to look at him. And this she now did again, working her way around the stout woman with the string bags.

Kate is not going to believe this, Megan said to herself. *Kate is simply not going to believe that I saw that boy in the Frankfurt airport.*

In fact, she was having difficulty believing, herself, that she and that boy had flown together on the same crowded commuter plane from London to Frankfurt. And, of course, that meant he had

3

been on his way to Heathrow Airport at the very same time Kate and her mother were delivering her there, too. It was just all too much.

Where he might be going now, however, she had no idea. Frankfurt was the jumping-off point for any number of cities: Budapest, Prague, both Berlins, Krakow, Bratislava, Moscow. All were possible destinations. She'd seen the names of these cities listed somewhere, along with flight numbers and times of departures, but had made no note of them. The plane for Budapest left at 5:10, which was the only time important for her to remember. That was now less than a half hour away.

That the boy might be going on to Budapest was highly improbable. But perhaps no more so than all the other improbable things that had happened in the last few weeks, and the even more improbable things that had happened in the last few days.

Of course, for months now her father had planned to attend that conference for scientists from all over the world to be held in Budapest. Fortunately, that event was working in well with two other scientific meetings, one in Helsinki and the other in Paris, which previously he had hoped, but had hardly expected, to attend. For the Budapest conference not only was he the only American scientist to be invited, but he had been asked to deliver a paper on one of his esoteric subjects. Megan remembered how pleased he had been. It was, he felt, another sign of improving relations between the Communists and the Free World—

particularly in the United States—because, as he pointed out, Russia, not Hungary, was the country really sponsoring the conference.

But no matter whose idea the conference was, no one could deny that whoever had done the inviting—Russia or Hungary—had known what he was about. Even so, it was hard for her to remember that the man she called "Daddy" was the nation's outstanding physicist in the field of cosmic radiation. And if this were not enough, there was the top secret work he did for the government and no one—well, hardly anyone—knew anything about that.

Certainly, at the time of the invitation and indeed for several months afterward, there had been no thought of her flying even as far as London with her father. The summer would pass, she had thought, with her taking classes mornings at the Art Students League, sketching in Central Park—the area right across from the Plaza Hotel was not only interesting but safe—playing tennis or swimming. Spending August in Maine with her family would be the best time of all.

It had taken Colonel Cade's transfer from New York City to London—which, of course, meant the transfer of the entire Cade ménage, including Kate who'd been her best friend at Miss Ivory's School, Kate's mother, four younger brothers and sisters and two standard French poodles—to start the wheels in motion for her to visit them.

The complexities of Megan's own family life had begun the second phase. While she was breakfasting with her parents one Sunday morning only a little over a month before, her mother had said to her father as if she were merely thinking aloud, "You know, Thomas, if Megan had something interesting to do while you were trotting all over Europe to your conferences, I'd take myself up to the shack and finish my book."

The shack, of course, wasn't really a shack at all but a small sturdy A-framed cottage in Maine looking out to Spain over several thousand miles of Atlantic Ocean. They'd spent part of every summer there as long as Megan could remember. As for the book her mother had so casually mentioned, *that* would be published by the Yale University Press as *the* definitive work on the Lepidoptera of the world.

Megan looked up from a perfectly poached egg atop a toasted English muffin crowned with deviled ham. For a scientist, her mother was a remarkably good cook. "What sort of interesting thing did you have in mind for me?"

"Didn't you have a letter from Kate inviting you to visit her in London sometime this summer?"

"Just last week."

Gillian More's gray blue eyes were smiling. "Probably more to the point, I have had a letter from Mrs. Cade seconding the invitation, though how anyone with five children would willingly ask for one more . . ."

Megan leaped up from her chair. "Mother! You're not serious! Daddy, would you let me, *really*?"

"It bears thinking about," her mother said.

"If it's all right with your mother, it's all right

with me. Without even trying, I can see you and Kate larking around London.''

Megan gave her mother, then her father, a strangling hug. "You are the best parents a girl ever had. Also the smartest, the most beautiful and most handsome.''

"Flattery will get you nowhere," Thomas More said, with a fake smug look. "Now before you start packing you'd better help your mother clear the table.''

Megan's mind darted from the scene in the sunny kitchen that looked out over the treetops of New York's Central Park to a scene in the large and rather murky kitchen of the Cades' apartment in London. She and Kate had been eating breakfast there two days before when the boy came with the telegram.

Not reassured by Kate's, "There's no black band around the envelope, so at least you know that no one's dead," Megan had shakily read it through, then handed it to her friend.

Kate let out a scream that woke up one of the poodles asleep under the table. "Your father wants you to join him in Budapest day after tomorrow, and you've only just got here! You can't! It's impossible!''

But, of course, it hadn't been. Everything her father's telegram had told her to do—from getting her Hungarian visa and the *forint* vouchers for a three-day stay, to making the proper airline reservations—she had done.

And here she was in the Frankfurt airport while

a voice over the loudspeaker announced in several languages that the flight to Budapest was boarding!

Time had passed more quickly than she thought. She took a quick look around. The boy in the brown raincoat, however, was nowhere to be seen. Nor was there any sign of him as she passed, along with a line of other passengers, through the door leading to the plane. Her stomach felt a little queer, the way it sometimes did when she was getting ready to take an examination in a subject in which she was not well prepared. The flight from London to Frankfurt had not so affected her, but then she was flying BEA. And British airlines, except for the accents of the pretty stewardesses, were scarcely different from those in America. She wished she could have stayed with BEA—they, too, flew to Budapest—but her father had told her to book passage on MALEV, the Hungarian line. Even the name MALEV sounded faintly sinister. Like malevolent, or malice, or malignant. She wondered how many other evil-sounding Hungarian words there were although she knew it was silly to think of things like that. Hungary welcomed foreign travelers. Hungarian citizens enjoyed more of the good life than the people of any other Soviet satellite, even of Russia itself.

Fortunately, the atmosphere inside the plane exuded no hint of any of the "mals." The stewardess to whom Megan showed her boarding pass looked scarcely older than Megan herself.

"You are American?" She spoke smilingly.

"Why, yes." Although at first startled at the

girl's near-perfect English, she smiled, too. "Does being an American really show?"

"One gets to know the traveling public." She nodded toward the interior of the aircraft. "You may sit anywhere you like."

The plane, which was roughly the size of the one in which she'd flown from London to Frankfurt and was likewise of a single class, was already more than half filled. However, to her disappointment, a quick but thorough search of the passengers on board revealed no sign of the boy in the brown raincoat.

There were no window seats available, so Megan chose one next to an elderly woman wearing a long black dress and a kind of shawl over her head. In her hands was a rosary made of large brown beads with a wooden crucifix which her fingers clutched nervously.

As the plane took off and the earth, shrouded in a soft rainy mist, slipped away from beneath them Megan wished she could say something to reassure her companion. But she feared *The Handy Hungarian Phrase Book* Kate Cade had given her (along with *The Handy Short Course in Hungarian History*) just before they had said good-bye at Heathrow wasn't going to be much help. For the second time that day, she got the book out of her purse and ran down a list of some of the phrases. "Good morning!" "Good evening!" "See you again, so long!" "Where is the snackbar, the airport, the cloakroom, the movies?" "A chemist's shop?" "Many thanks!" "Don't mention it!" and "How do you say it in Hungarian?"

She giggled softly to herself. The phrases and questions were almost identical to those in the back of her French book and were unfortunately the kind of thing one rarely said or asked. But even if any had been appropriate for this occasion she would not have dared to try to speak such a mouthful of consonants as *"Hogyan mondjak ezt magyarul?"* The phonetic pronunciation that followed was no easier to say than the original.

She put the book face down on her lap, looked at her watch and then glanced around her. It scarcely seemed possible that they had been airborne for almost an hour. In the meantime, early nightfall had closed in and encapsulated them.

Though the elderly woman next to her still clutched her rosary, her eyes were closed and her expression peaceful. For the barest moment Megan thought she might have died of fright, then a gentle snore reassured her. The passengers across the aisle had also nodded off to sleep and others, several rows ahead, were folding coats or sweaters into little packets on which to rest their heads. An outraged baby who had been crying had either been fed or cried himself to sleep.

Indeed, it seemed as if everyone on the plane had wrapped himself in a quiet cocoon of his own making in order to prepare for whatever might be awaiting him in Budapest. Except for her. Though an element of unreality was all-pervasive, never had she felt more wakeful, more wide-eyed or alert. Every sense seemed sharpened, honed, refined to a pitch that she had never experienced before. The pungent smell of a freshly peeled orange mingled with the acrid, throat-hurting smell of burning pipe tobacco—so unlike the fragrant aroma of Balkan Sobranie which was her father's favorite blend.

Although only four days had elapsed since she and her father had parted in London—she to go home with the Cades and he to take the next plane for Budapest—how much she would have to tell him! About the play at the Aldwych Theatre, the Royal Shakespeare Company in *The Taming of the Shrew*, the day of sight-seeing with Kate from the top of a great, lumbering double-decker bus and, of course, about the interesting boy in the brown raincoat.

Then, as if the thought of him had worked a magic spell, the door to the pilot's compartment opened and he appeared. Smiling faintly, he swung down the aisle. Closer . . . closer . . . closer . . . He was taller than she'd thought and even more good looking. Though how that could be . . . Her heart gave a little thump of excitement. If that *Handy Hungarian Phrase Book* had something useful in it, like "Won't you sit down and let's get acquainted," she would have tackled it, no matter how foolish the sounds that came out.

But better still, perhaps he would sit down by her. Fortunately, the aisle seat had remained free. Even if he did not sit down, he might smile. It was inconceivable, when she was so aware of him, that he could not even be aware that she existed.

Now he was abreast of her, but his eyes were looking straight ahead. And now he had passed her by!

How could he?

But on the other hand, how could he not? She

11

wasn't beautiful. At least, not yet—though she felt that someday she might be. She could feel it working inside her, trying to come out. Perhaps his mind was occupied with some weighty subject. She could understand *that*. When her father was deep in thought, sometimes he forgot not only where he was but whether or not he had had his dinner. The night before they'd left for London, he'd come out of his study and tactfully inquired.

Or the boy, though he looked no more than twenty, might be a courier for his government— whatever government that might be—carrying documents of vital importance from one country to another.

She smiled at the liveliness of her imagination, though she was glad she had it. Whether she decided to become a writer, an artist or both, it would come in handy. Even so, the thought that he was *somebody* would not go away. If he were not, why should he have emerged so nonchalantly from the cockpit of the plane where ordinary passengers were not allowed? And if he had been in there talking to the pilots of a Hungarian airline, would he not be speaking Hungarian?

Her head began to spin. But if he did not speak English, too, why would he be reading *The London Times* and *Newsweek*, which were most certainly printed in English?

With no answers to her questions, she turned again to her *Handy Hungarian Phrase Book*. As difficult as the language was, a few words might still come in handy.

2
The Meeting
At The Metropole

MEGAN COULD FEEL A SUDDEN SPASM in her stomach as the plane lost altitude, shuddered, then leveled off again.

The hands of her watch pointed to six-fifteen. Somehow it seemed later than that. Rather, because of the rain, it seemed to be no time at all. Driplets of water crawled down the window pane and disappeared into nothingness. The interior lights of the plane had been turned on soon after takeoff, but they were no longer so bright and, occasionally, flickered fitfully making reading impossible.

Once again, the plane lost altitude. Now, too, as the whining of the jet engines was growing louder, Megan could both see and feel the passengers bestir themselves and begin to gather together their possessions. A voice saying something she could not understand crackled over the loudspeaker and the air of expectancy increased. The stewardesses, who had been walking up and down the aisle looking to see that seat belts were fastened and seats in upright position, sat down themselves.

The plane bounced unnervingly as the wheels hit the ground and shot down the invisible runway in a torrent of noise. Earlier, Megan had reached for the hand of the elderly woman next to her—whether to comfort or be comforted, she could not be sure—and she continued to hold it tightly until the plane, like a giant bird of prey suddenly tamed, taxied for an interminable distance and came to a meek and silent halt.

As people began pushing down the aisle, Megan stood up and put on her raincoat, buttoning it all the way. Rain would make no difference to her hair. Straight and shining black, she still wore it as she had worn it when she was a child: shoulder length and bangs cut straight across.

She retrieved her only piece of luggage, a small blue suitcase, from under the seat; hung her camera, safe in its waterproof case, around her neck and her purse over her shoulder; and moved out into the aisle.

At the door the stewardess smiled and said, "Good-bye."

"Perhaps I should say 'hello' to Budapest."

"That would be nice," the stewardess said, and turned her attention to the next passenger.

Rain was falling steadily but not heavily as Megan walked down the steps of the plane and onto the wet and glistening tarmac. She could see dozens of dim shapes ahead of her, streaming toward the lights of what must be a long low wing of the airport. Inside the building, she continued to follow those who were not waiting for luggage to arrive and moved up a flight of stairs where a soldier in a dirty-colored khaki uniform directed them to a long table behind which were two other soldiers similarly garbed. One was peering into opened suitcases spread along its length while the other examined passports and visas. Though some people seemed to have their passports returned promptly and their belongings examined only cursorily or not at all, others were diverted to one side where their apparent nervousness added to her own growing unease.

Though the young man at the travel agency in London had assured her she would have no trouble and that all her papers were in order, how could she be sure? Why should a person have to have a visa to enter one country but not another? Why could people go freely into Austria but not into Hungary? Why into Yugoslavia, but not into Czechoslovakia? Why had she had to "buy" so many dollars' worth of Hungarian money for each day she planned to be in the country?

Now, there were only three more people ahead of her. Two. Then one. The young soldier who took her passport was young with a blotchy red complexion. He took it gravely, turned a page, stared at the photograph again. It did make her look, Megan thought, "not quite all there." But even as unflattering as it was, she didn't see how he could deny that the girl in the picture, with the straight black hair, wide-set eyes and quirky dimple in her chin, was the same girl that stood before him. He flipped another page, frowned when he saw that the visa had been stapled to a page in the passport and carefully pried it up with the point of his penknife. Another quick look and he seemed mentally to weigh and measure her against her height of five feet five and weight of one hundred and eighteen pounds.

"You are staying in Hungary how long?"

"I'll be here three days. My father is in Budapest now. He is coming to meet me." The words came out in a rush because it was so good to be communicating again. Except for that brief exchange with the stewardess, she'd talked to no one at all. "I don't see my father yet, but I know he's in there." She nodded her head toward the next room, where the man who had been just ahead of her in line was being rapturously embraced by his wife while a small boy clung to each of his legs.

The young soldier made no move to stamp her visa but with something of a gesture put it to one side and pointed to the blue suitcase at her feet. "You will open, please."

Megan picked it up and placed it on the counter but before she could dial the combination lock that opened it, the young soldier was pushed peremptorily aside by a stout, heavy-jowled man with a bristling gray mustache who quickly stamped her visa and returned it with the passport. "Pass through," he said curtly. "No need to open the suitcase. Pass through."

It had all happened so quickly that she barely had time to utter a startled "thank you" before moving into the adjoining room. Everywhere there was a good deal of rapid talking and laughing. But her father . . . where was he? Not only was he taller than average, but with his young face beneath a shock of hair once as black as her own but already streaked with silver, he would stand out anywhere. People called him "distinguished," but that only made him laugh. "I refuse to look distinguished," he always said, "until I'm fifty years old"—and he wouldn't be that age for another six years.

The blue suitcase banged at her knees as she roamed around the room. A hard knot formed in her throat and she felt the pressure of tears against her eyelids. Determinedly, she held them back. Just because she didn't see him, that didn't mean he wasn't there. But as the room began to clear, she had to admit her self-delusion. The important thing to do was sit down and think quietly about the course she should take. She sank down in the nearest chair, not noticing a nearby ashtray filled with smoldering, evil-smelling cigarettes. Before she could move, a spell of coughing seized her.

"Here. Let me take that thing away."

Through a haze of tears and lashes, she looked up. The boy in the brown raincoat was standing over her and the ashtray was no longer there.

Afterward, she was to think how crazy it was that the first thing she said to him was, "I'm not crying."

"Of course not." His voice was grave.

Her "thank you" was as much for his seeming to understand that girls didn't cry as it was for the very white, still folded handkerchief he gave her.

"You are waiting for someone who has not come?"

She nodded. "My father." It was hard to keep the tremor from her voice. "I arrived just a little while ago, from London."

The boy's eyes were such a dark blue they seemed almost black. "I know. I saw you there."

"I saw you, too." Despite her worry, she managed a little smile.

"Then we are not strangers. My name is András Nador." The slight courteous gesture that he made, the barest bending at the waist and inclination of his head, was something like a bow yet could not really be called a bow at all.

"I am Megan More."

Again the little gesture. "If you will allow me, I will take you to your father's hotel."

"It's the Metropole. I . . . I don't know where it is."

"It is familiar to me. We have newer, finer hotels, some with the baths for which Budapest is so well known, but the Metropole is very old. Very famous. Many important visitors stay there. Your father is a famous visitor?"

"In our country . . . in the United States . . ." She paused, wondering if it would appear ill-mannered to say how famous her father really was. Only a few months before, his picture, superimposed upon a drawing of spaceships, planes and rockets twirling through the heavens, had been on the cover of *Time* magazine. The story inside told about his research in the field of cosmic radiation and its uses. There had also been an oblique reference to a discovery that would give the United States a new and super-sophisticated secret weapon. He had been furious about that mention, but even more furious about the magazine's dragging in the fact that he was a direct lineal descendant of Sir Thomas More and calling him "America's man for all seasons."

"Well?" said András, who was still waiting for her to answer.

"Well, in the United States he is a little famous," Megan said, bringing herself back with a little laugh. "Hardly anyone understands, though, so I don't try to explain. But he's a physicist—and he does research on cosmic radiation. Solar energy. Things like that."

"Men with good minds, like that of your father, are welcome in Budapest. So many people who could have made Hungary great are . . . gone."

"Gone?"

Almost as if he were talking to himself András, eyes looking not at her but seemingly into some limitless void, continued. "During the Second Great War, four hundred thousand Hungarian Jews—80 percent of all in the country—perished in gas chambers. Though I was not yet alive, I have heard that during the seven-week siege of Budapest, only a month before VE day when peace was declared through all of Europe, bands of killers—young people little more than children—roamed through the streets of Budapest, massacring Jews and even those suspected of being anti-Nazis. Later, in 1956, when the country could stand no more and the Revolution came, two hundred thousand Hungarians went into exile never to return."

Megan shivered. "I . . . I'm sorry."

András smiled, returning to himself. "It is not your fault. And, besides, I talk too much about the troubles of Hungary when we should be thinking of your father." He glanced at his watch. "Still, not too much time has gone by. A busy man can be detained. Besides, the rain. See?" He inclined his head toward an outside door, through which a number of people with dripping umbrellas had just entered. "In Budapest when it rains, taxicabs are difficult to get. In London, also. Perhaps in the United States of America, with so many automobiles everywhere, it is not true. Yes?"

Except for an occasional involuted sentence the pattern of which she found herself wanting to follow, his English scarcely differed from her own.

"It is true, yes. Everywhere in the United States—though New York City is the worst—taxicabs are difficult to get when it rains."

"Perhaps I shall be lucky in finding one to take you to your hotel."

"But should I wait here? What if my father came and didn't find me?"

"With a girl old enough to travel so far, he would not worry." He paused. "I *think* he would not worry, though how old you are I do not know."

Megan ignored the invitation to explore her age. Somehow, it did not seem right. In fact, now that she was face to face with him—or almost so, since he had sat down in the nearest chair and pulled it toward her as he talked—in some way she could not explain he seemed older. Perhaps it was the presence of two tiny lines already etched at the corners of his mouth, or the way he sometimes tensed the muscles along the angle of his jaw.

He got up suddenly. "It is, of course, what you wish to do."

"If you could call the hotel . . . find out if he's left."

"A most sensible idea. I should have thought of that myself. Please wait here."

She watched as he crossed the room and turned a corner out of sight. The last of the passengers who had been with her on the flight from Frankfurt had long since disappeared into the rainy and now dark night. Little pools of water on the floor were the only evidence of a succession of new arrivals who had moved on into other areas of the airport.

Her heart seemed to keep leaden time with the movements of the minute hand of the big clock on the wall. Five minutes. Ten minutes. If he did not come back, how long should she wait before starting off to find her father on her own? She fought down a growing feeling of uneasiness, knowing she must act sensibly. Her father would not have allowed her to come so far if he had not been confident that she could take care of herself if an emergency arose. And even if there was something strange about the boy, András—it was the first time she had thought his name—and the way their paths kept crossing, she felt in some inexplicable way that their meeting was meant to be. In spite of

21

her tiredness and the queerness of everything, that romantic expression "meant to be" struck her as amusing.

The feeling was not to last. András had appeared around the corner shaking his head. "No luck. The storm has been very heavy. I cannot get through to the hotel. We had better see about a taxi." He picked up Megan's suitcase and with the other hand cupped lightly around her elbow guided her toward the door.

Outside the rain was falling steadily, beating in under the extension of the roof where they stood. "Someone is always coming to the airport, so we should get a taxi soon. You can recognize one by the sign *'Szabad'* on top." He peered into the darkness through which the watery gleam of approaching headlights was managing to penetrate. "Yes. One comes now. It is a *kis*, but that is all right."

"A what?"

The boy laughed. It was a pleasant sound. "A *kis*, but it is not what you are thinking. A Hungarian *kis* has nothing to do with kissing, though that is all right, too. It means only that it is a *small* cab. It carries only three passengers, plus the driver."

Someone waiting for a taxi ahead of them took that *kis*, however, and another ten minutes passed before another pulled into the curb. When no passenger emerged, Megan's last hope that her father might still arrive to meet her vanished.

The *kis*, indeed, was small. With András and his flight bag and Megan with her suitcase, camera and purse, it was hard to see where a third person might fit in. The *kis* was also fast. They rounded a corner with such speed that Megan found herself even closer to András than she had been before. A second later, a zigzag of white lightning sundered the heavens and a clap of thunder reverberated with such force that she buried her face against his chest.

. She raised her head ashamedly. "Really, I'm not afraid of storms. It . . . it's just that all that noise startled me."

"Sometimes when it thunders like that we say the Turks are coming."

"The Turks . . ." She spoke slowly, trying to remember what *The Handy Short Course in Hungarian History* had said about them, but it wasn't any use.

"It is a joke. About the Turks. Hungarians are fond of jokes. Maybe it is a way of letting the steam out of the teakettle. Though it is only Magyars to whom Hungary belongs, everyone— Romans, Avars, Huns, Turks—everyone comes to Hungary in time."

"And the Russians . . ." It was the wrong thing to say. Too late she remembered that that was what the Revolution of 1956 was all about. Though the Russians "liberated" Hungary at the end of World War II, they had stayed on to create conditions so intolerable that two hundred thousand people had fled the country.

Fortunately, András seemed not to have heard. Turned toward the window, he was rubbing his hand against the mist on the pane. It made no appreciable difference. The rain was still beating down with such force that it was impossible to see

23

anything more than that the highway on which they had been traveling had given way to a boulevard of tremendous width with parked cars huddling against the curbings like dark, cowed beasts.

"We will be at your hotel very soon. There we will say 'good-bye' " There was an air of finality in his words.

"You . . . you have been very kind."

"Not at all."

The taxi came to a stop, furrowing through a churning river of water along the curb. Megan opened her purse. "I haven't any money, just these *forint* voucher things. Or, maybe, American dollars might do?"

"Oh, American dollars would do very well. We like them very much in Hungary. Also we like British pounds, French *francs*, Austrian *schillings*, German *marks*. That is because *outside* Hungary, in the West that is, no one likes *forints* at all. One *forint* buys nothing. Not even a cup of coffee. But that is all quite beside the point. It is not for you to pay."

It was no time for arguing. He had already paid the driver and, her blue suitcase in hand, was already hurrying her into the lobby of the hotel.

"You will be all right now. So I will say good-bye." Once again, he made the courteous little gesture that was something like a bow yet was not a bow at all.

"My father . . . I thought you might wait to see if he is here."

"He will be here, I am sure. Goodnight."

"But my father would like to thank you . . ."

Already he had turned and was walking swiftly toward the door. She looked after him until he was gone, then around the near-empty lobby of the hotel. Huge and high ceilinged, it stretched away on one side into a dim vastness furnished with crouching sofas and chairs where a scattering of people sat. Through large double doors she could hear the sound of a violin playing gypsy music and see people dining. The hotel desk—long, ornately carved with a marble pillar at either end—was closer by. Behind it two men—one young, one old—watched as she approached.

"Thomas More . . . he is registered here?" The inside of her mouth felt as if it were lined with cotton.

"Ah, yes. Dr. More. A most distinguished visitor." The older of the two men spoke. Closely spaced eyes in a bony and pallid face examined her. "You are his daughter?"

Megan nodded.

"Then to register, please." He turned a large, leather-bound book toward her as he spoke.

Although Megan grasped the pen firmly she had difficulty keeping her signature, always scrawly, firmly on the line.

"Now your passport, please."

Megan took it from the secret compartment in her purse, then watched with growing uneasiness as the bony one examined it and then deposited it in a safe on the wall.

"Why are you doing that?" She could not help but feel alarmed. Practically the last thing her father had said to her before they'd parted was to keep her passport with her at all times.

"All visitors to the People's Democracy of Hungary must be registered with the police, but that," he added, "is merely a formality. The custom is practiced throughout much of Europe. The passport is merely kept in the safe for safekeeping. *Safe*-keeping."

Because he'd smiled when he repeated the words, Megan supposed it was one of the Hungarian jokes András had told her about. If so, she thought poorly of it. For one day, she'd had quite enough. Fortunately, it did seem to be about over. In response to a snap of the man's fingers a boy appeared out of the lobby's shadowy depths, was given an order and picked up her suitcase. Trotting ahead of her, he moved toward a bank of elevators she had not seen before. There, moving from one to another, he pushed buttons until minutes later a lighted cage appeared. Heavily grilled and cavernous, it creakingly ascended. The boy smiled reassuringly. "Very old hotel, very old elevator. But also very safe. We get off now, please."

She followed the boy halfway down the long, wide corridor that lay ahead, stopping when he did before a pair of high double doors with crystal knobs. He tapped once, lightly, the second time more loudly, then with an apologetic glance, a third time more loudly still.

Pressing her hand hard against her chest, Megan then knew for sure what all along she'd half suspected. *She never should have left the airport. She should have waited until her father came, even if she'd had to wait half the night.*

When the door opened she could hear, as if with another part of her being, her breath drawing in and her voice crying out "Daddy!"

But it was not until she was inside the room with the door closed and her face muffled against the warmth of her father's chest that she allowed herself to become a little girl again.

"You didn't come," she whimpered. "Daddy, you didn't *come*!"

"I know . . . I know . . ."

Half-angry with him for the worry he had caused her, she pushed herself away. "But why, Daddy? Why didn't you meet me, when you said you would?"

He gave her a queer close look as if to make certain it was really she who stood there, then glanced behind him into the room where a huge man with the bland face of a Humpty Dumpty was rising ponderously from a sofa. "Perhaps this gentleman here can answer that. I didn't know that you were coming."

3
Introducing
Dr. Dozsás

THE LARGE, HIGH-WINDOWED ROOM tilted to one side, then began spinning like a pinwheel. When it stopped, the fat man was right side up again and she was still standing near the doorway, her father's arm around her.

"You're all right?"

Megan nodded, vaguely aware the never before had she seen her father's face so bleached of color.

"Let's get that wet raincoat off you. Then you'd better start at the beginning."

"When . . . when you sent the telegram telling me to come . . . I mean . . ." She paused to correct herself. "I mean, when *someone* did." Although she gave the fat man a baleful glance, she could feel him beaming upon her as if she were a clever child.

"Ah, indeed, and I do fear that it was I." The voice that issued from a mouth much too small for

29

the dimensions of his face was as clear and resonant as a bell.

Thomas More waved a hand as if brushing away a troublesome insect. To Megan, he said "Go on."

"I've still got the telegram, if you want to see it." She dug it out of her purse and handed it to him. Having read it so many times her mind was able to recall each word as her father's eyes scanned the rather crumpled sheet of yellow paper. BUDAPEST BEAUTIFUL STOP JOIN ME TUESDAY JUNE NINE STOP WILL MEET MALEV FLIGHT SEVEN ELEVEN ARRIVING NINETEEN HOURS THIRTY-FIVE MINUTES STOP OBTAIN HUNGARIAN VISA AND PICK UP PREPAID AIRLINE TICKETS PLUS FORINTS AT BREEDLOVE TRAVEL AGENCY LTD NEW BOND STREET STOP NOTE CAREFULLY DEPARTURE TIMES BOTH LONDON AND FRANKFURT STOP DO NOT DISAPPOINT LOVE FATHER.

"You thought this was from me?" There was both disapproval and disbelief in his voice.

"Of course! Or else I wouldn't have come." She couldn't help feeling hurt.

"And Colonel Cade? Mrs. Cade? They raised no questions?"

"Colonel Cade wasn't home. He'd gone to Paris for a meeting. And Mrs. Cade . . ." She felt herself flushing. Now that she knew her father hadn't sent that telegram, it didn't sound like him at all. For one thing, she always called him "Daddy." *Never* "Father." And in every letter he ever had written her, "Daddy" was the way he signed his name.

She continued lamely. "At first, Mrs. Cade thought it . . . well, unusual that you sent a telegram instead of calling me long distance. Then we decided that you might have called the night before when all of us were gone. The younger children had gone with us to the theater, too, so there wasn't even a sitter there."

Suddenly, the fat man came twinkling toward them on small, neatly shod feet. "Dr. More, please! Please, let us not have an inquisition of your daughter whom, incidentally, I have not had the pleasure of meeting." He paused, waiting expectantly until Thomas More performed the introduction—one that Megan knew only instinctive politeness forced him to make.

"Megan, this is Dr. Janos Dozsás, Undersecretary in Charge of Foreign Affairs of the People's Democracy of Hungary. Mr. Secretary, my daughter, Megan More."

Dozsás bowed sweepingly, in the process seizing Megan's unsuspecting hand which he pressed moistly to his lips.

"*Mademoiselle, j'suis charmé*. And now that we have met, let us adjourn to my favorite restaurant in all of Budapest, the Citadella. A most unusual place, it is built within the ancient walls of the fortress the Austrians erected to dominate Budapest. There we shall have veal stuffed with goose liver. Or perhaps, beef ragout in Hungarian fashion, again with the goose liver, but prepared flambé at the table. For dessert, I think, a *dobostorta*—a cake of many delicious layers, with a hard burnt-sugar topping. Or, even better yet, a *turoscsusza*. It is said of the *turoscsusza*, it is too good for angels but not too good for Magyars. Nor too good for our young American friend whom, with so much planning and ingenuity, we have brought to join her eminent father. So do not worry! Ask no questions! Enjoy the surprise that has been prepared for you!''

Megan scarcely dared to look at her father whose complexion had turned from that of a blanched almond to an angry red. "You are talking the most complete and arrant nonsense. I shall not even ask for an explanation of this telegram. The first thing tomorrow morning, I will make representation to the American Consul. After that, my daughter and I will take the first plane out of Budapest.''

"My very dear sir! I am sorry that you have reacted so.'' A sibilant henlike clucking sound that women sometimes make when they are sorry emerged from the small "O" of his mouth. "Those who were . . . shall I say . . . in charge were mainly thinking how delighted you would be to have the company of your charming daughter while you are here in our city. And they were thinking, too, of the rich cultural experience it would be for your daughter. I ask you, how many young ladies of her age have the opportunity to learn, first hand, of our country's customs? Or to see how excellent is the life now enjoyed by the fortunate ones who live in the People's Democracy of Hungary? This is not even to speak of the additional pleasure of hearing her father address the greatest of scientific conferences ever held in Eastern Europe.''

Thomas More shook his head again as if to flick away an annoying insect. ''There is nothing you can say that will excuse bringing a sixteen-year-old girl halfway across the continent of Europe on false pretenses. And alone.''

''But not alone!'' The Undersecretary held up a plump well-manicured forefinger as if it were an exclamation point. ''I do not think for a moment that she should be called 'alone.' Someone, I believe, was at all times very near, watching to see that no harm could come. I suspect that it was a very attractive 'someone.' '' He turned to Megan with an actorish bow and a sly smile. ''You need not answer, my dear. As the father of two young girls, I appreciate your possible embarrassment.''

''I will listen to no more. Now, if you will please go and leave my daughter and me.''

''My dear Dr. More, go I cannot until you understand how unfortunate it would be if you left Budapest before the conference is over. You cannot know how we are counting on you. To speak, that is. Perhaps, instead of the three of us going out to dine your daughter would leave us so we could talk frankly. After her long journey she cannot help but be most tired. Then I would be able to make my position clear.''

Although the Undersecretary's face had not lost its bland Humpty Dumpty expression, his voice had taken on a wheedling tone. ''You know how long and difficult were the negotiations your Mr. Kissinger went through with our . . . er . . . com-

33

patriots in Hanoi before the immoral and imperialistic war in Vietnam could be ended. Our . . . er . . . negotiations need not be so long nor so difficult. Scarcely could they be called negotiations, but talk I think we must."

There was a long silence before she heard her father say, "Megan, if you don't mind . . . for only a few minutes, please." He nodded his head toward the adjoining bedroom.

She would have remonstrated if she had thought it would do any good. But ever since she was about three years old, she'd been able to tell when her father's mind was made up. As she became older, her mother had explained (not unsympathetically) that when he seemed to be the most unreasonable it was merely the "Thomas More" in him coming out. When he was convinced he was right, her mother said, he was as unlikely to yield or change his mind as the first Thomas More had been. Over four hundred years before, *that* Thomas More had come up against King Henry VIII. Though once Henry's friend, he'd allowed himself to be beheaded as a traitor rather than take an oath acknowledging that the King and not the Pope had authority over the English Church. Glancing at her father's set jaw she wondered if he had any awareness that *she* might have a bit of "Moreishness" in her, too.

Nonetheless, when her father once again asked her to go into the bedroom, she went. Still, she was not above leaving the door slightly ajar, nor was her father above closing it only a second later.

She listened at the keyhole through which, though it was large, she could hear nothing at all.

Successful eavesdropping was a phenomenon reserved only for books and movies. She considered lying on the floor and listening through a crack at the bottom of the door but discarded the idea. How ignominious to be found there if her father should suddenly open the door!

She switched on an old-fashioned-looking television set on a table in the corner of the room, but nothing happened. Not a squeak of a sound nor the flicker of a picture. She turned it off, listened once again at the keyhole, then threw herself down on one of the beds. "Five minutes," she said aloud. "I'll give him five minutes. Then I'm going to open that door and find out what's happening out there."

And she would have, too, had she not closed her eyes just a minute to rest them. But it had been a long day and the night before she and Kate had talked until almost morning.

When she awoke the room, except for a sliver of light coming through a crack under the door, was in darkness. She sat up, aware that her father, presumably, though it seemed in Hungary anything could happen, had covered her with a light blanket. At any rate, it was her father who was sound asleep in the next bed, a fact she determined by turning on a light by the bed and taking a good look at him.

She put a tentative hand on his shoulder with the thought of awakening him, then drew it back as he turned uneasily and muttered something she could not understand. Morning was now only a few hours away, and that would be time enough to find out what had happened between him and

Humpty Dumpty. She got her nightgown and toilet case out of her suitcase but decided there was no point in unpacking anything more. Although it was too bad to be leaving Budapest without seeing anything but the airport and one hotel, she still would have rather a lot to tell Kate Cade when she got back to London.

When she opened her eyes the sun was streaming into the room and the bed next to her was empty. And from the bathroom, which adjoined the sitting room on the other side of the hall, she could hear the sounds of water pipes rumbling.

Although her father had been known to occupy a bathroom indefinitely, he appeared a little later, shaved and dressed except for his shirt. He was smiling. "Good morning, sleepy head. So you decided to wake up, after all."

"You should have waked me last night after Mr. Undersecretary What's-His-Name left." Megan sat up in bed, pulling the sheet up under her chin.

"You were sleeping so soundly, I hadn't the heart. Though I did worry about your not having had any dinner."

"I wasn't hungry last night, but this morning . . ." As if to prove the truth of her statement, her stomach growled so ominously that they both had to laugh.

"Good. I've ordered breakfast for eight o'clock so it should be along soon."

As they'd talked, her father had put on a blue and white striped Brooks Brothers shirt—it was one she'd given him for Christmas a year before and had cost eighteen dollars—and was knotting a plain blue knit tie.

"Do you want me to go with you to tell the American Consul what happened?"

Although Thomas More's fingers went on almost automatically knotting his tie and buttoning down the tabs of his shirt, Megan looked guiltily away. Watching his reflection in the mirror she had seen, or did she only think she saw, a shadow cross his face. "I've changed my mind about going to the Consul."

"But last night, you said . . ."

"I know," he began, but paused when a tap came at the door of their suite. "Breakfast first, then I'll tell you why I've changed my mind."

Megan sniffed appreciatively as the waiter trundled the table into their sitting room. Salami, sliced paper thin, and enough on the serving plate to feed a family of four! Crusty rolls, cheese and jam and a steaming pot of tea. When, between them, they had devoured it all Megan said, "I still don't understand. Last night you were angry enough to pop, yet this morning you aren't angry any more."

"Oh, but I am. I don't think I'm ever going to recover from the shock of seeing you standing outside the door of a hotel in Budapest when I thought you were safe in the bosom of the Cade family in London. It's just that I don't think it would be wise to make an international incident out of it."

"I don't see how . . ."

"Dominoes." He spoke carefully, almost as if

he had rehearsed what he was going to say. "If I report the matter to the American Consul here, he informs the State Department. Washington then complains not only to the Hungarian government but to Moscow. You must remember that Dozsás is no fool in spite of his silly ways. He's not operating without the full knowledge and consent of someone considerably higher up—probably a man named Boris Bolonski. And you can be certain that neither of them dreamed up the scheme of bringing you here without some pretty strong nudging from Big Brother. When the Kremlin fiddles—if it *is* the Kremlin—Hungary dances."

Thomas More got up, walked over to the window and looked out for so long a time Megan thought he had forgotten her. Then he turned, resuming the same careful tone as before. "For almost the last thousand years, there has not been a country in Europe that has been overrun, fought over, and plundered more often than Hungary. Now it is Russia who, having supposedly 'liberated' Hungary at the end of the war and having put down the revolution in 1956 when the people could stand no more, calls the shots."

Megan shivered, remembering the way András had looked when he told the horror of the revolution and the two hundred thousand Hungarians who had gone into exile. What a strange boy he was—and how hard to tell what "side" he was on.

"Since then, the people have been trying hard. Doing their best to get along. If this means 'getting along'—accommodating—with Russia, that is what they are going to do. Remember, though, that everyone you meet wears a mask. It is impossible to see the face behind it. Take the man who brought our breakfast, or the boy who carried your suitcase last night. Maybe both of them are loyal members of the Communist Party. Maybe Communism has made their life better than it ever was before. On the other hand, some people prize their personal freedom more than they do the benefits of the Communist State.''

"But what about us?'' Megan asked shakily. She was beginning to feel that she was playing a part in a low budget movie, one with a "Parental Guidance'' listing. "What if something happens to us while this game . . . this game of dominoes is going on?''

"Not likely.'' Her father's grin was as unexpected as it was reassuring. "I didn't mean to sound so melodramatic, but the truth is that in spite of some rather high-handed meddling for which I don't understand the reason, they just wouldn't dare.''

"I'm still not sure I like it here.''

"Oh, you'll like it. You recall I spent three days here in Budapest before the conference opened just as an ordinary sightseer. Maybe not an 'ordinary' one, because our friend Dr. Dozsás has been put in charge of . . . shall I say . . . my indoctrination. Budapest is a beautiful city. The people are as warm and handsome as any I've ever met. Because no Hungarian expects a foreigner to learn his language, which is one of the most difficult on earth, a good many speak English. There's also a lot of history lying around for anyone that's interested. As for the conference, the speakers so far have all been excellent. The best paper yesterday was presented by a woman, Dr. Iva Pretalova, who has been doing some remarkable work on DNA. Today, I'm looking forward to hearing a man from the University of Krakow speak on interplanetary communication.''

Megan waggled her head as Bernie, the family basset, did when shaking water from his ears. ''How did you and Mama, who are both so smart, happen to beget anyone like me?''

''A genetic freak,'' Thomas More said, and grinned at his daughter in a special way he had. Megan grinned back, reflecting that the nicest thing about her family was that they could joke about her scientific ineptness—though it wasn't really all that funny to look through a microscope and never see anything more interesting than the reflection of her eyelashes; or, when looking through binoculars, to get so excited that her breath fogged the lens. The only abstract concepts her mind could encompass at all were in the field of art—and even there, she belonged to the *trompe l'oeil* school of Harnett and Peto and all that crowd, who could draw every vein in a leaf, every eyelash on an eye and every fine grain in a piece of wood.

Suddenly, she didn't feel like joking any more. ''I still don't know what we're going to do.''

''Just what I'd planned all along. Deliver my paper as scheduled on Friday morning, the last day of the conference. I'll finish in plenty of time to check out of the hotel and catch a twelve-ten flight to Helsinki. The only change is that now you will be with me. In Helsinki, we'll get in touch with the Cades telling them when to expect you and put you on a plane for London." He glanced at his watch. "If I'm going to get to the university in time to hear Lazlo Ferenc, I'd better hurry. Want to come along?"

"I don't think I'd get a lot out of it. My Polish or whatever is a little rusty."

"Don't be a goose. They use the same system at the conference they do at the United Nations. You put on earphones and listen to an immediate translation in the language of your choice."

Megan shook her head. "Thanks, but I'd rather stay here and write to Kate. I promised I would, even if she doesn't get the letter until I'm back in London. After I do that, well . . . I don't know."

"Why don't you stick around the hotel—not go out at all? I think I'd be easier in my mind if I knew exactly where you were. I'll be back about noon. After that, we'll go to that restaurant Dozsás was salivating over last night and then go sight-seeing." As Thomas More talked, he was also preparing to leave. He checked the inside breast pocket of his coat to make sure his passport and billfold were there, put loose change and the red Swiss army knife he always carried with him into an outside pocket, and distributed his pipe, tobacco pouch and handkerchief in other inner and outer pockets. "You've got some *forints*? You'll need a bundle of them, because they're only worth about three cents apiece, even if you buy postcards and stamps."

"I've got lots."

"And American dollars?"

"I've some of those, too. Mrs. Cade said they always came in handy." András had said that, too. It was strange how thoughts of him came creeping in.

"You'll need dollars if you buy anything at the tourist shop. Hungarian money won't buy anything there. But for God's sake don't buy anything that won't fit in your suitcase. I don't want to be going back to the States with a nine by twelve rug rolled up under my arm."

"Don't worry, I won't." Megan kissed her father's cheek which smelled pleasantly of shaving soap and Brut.

At the door he paused. "You're sure you'll be all right?"

"Of course. Didn't I come all the way from London alone?"

It was the wrong thing to say, for a shadow crossed his face. "That's right. You did. I'm not likely to forget that." Then with a quick grin, he closed the door behind him.

4
A View From
The Hills of Buda

HAVING JUST FINISHED WRITING Kate a
bone-chilling account of all that had happened
since they'd said good-bye at Heathrow Airport
just the day before, she almost jumped out of her
skin when a small tap came at the door.

She squeaked out a cautious, "Who is it,
please?" only to feel exceedingly foolish when a
soft-spoken voice identified itself as the waiter
come to retrieve the breakfast table.

The waiter, in fact, turned out to be the same
one who had delivered the Mores' breakfast
earlier that morning. Megan had noticed him
then. A small man with a sharp ferretlike face and
shoulders that sloped away under a starched white
coat that was much too large for him. Not exactly
a reassuring type.

Megan drew back as he sidled past her into the
room and with a furtive glance began rather

noisily stacking dishes and silverware. However, instead of leaving after he had finished the task he stood, eyes cast down, as if waiting for something. She scarcely thought he could be expecting another tip—she had seen her father tip him that morning when he had brought their break-fast—but when he continued to stand there the silence so embarrassed her that she took a hun-dred-*forint* note from her purse—she had to remind herself that although it sounded like a lot it still amounted only to about thirty cents in American money—and held it toward him.

Almost with a look of revulsion, he brushed it aside. "Money, no! I wait, because I do not know how to say . . ." A quick look over his shoulder. "You are American. I am friend. I help. Olka, chambermaid . . ." Now even his whisper was shaky. "She pretends she has not English. Do not believe. She understands. She spies. She tells. *I* am friend." By the time he had finished, his voice had almost dropped off to nothing and, quickly trundling the table before him, he skittered through the door just ahead of a plump pretty girl with reddish gold braids who entered carrying a pile of bed linen and towels.

With an apologetic little smile and saying something that sounded like "you rag galt," she disappeared into the bedroom from which shortly issued a gay little song mingled with the snap of sheets being spread on the beds.

Megan looked after her doubtfully. *A spy?* It was hard to believe. A much more likely candidate was the furtive little man in white. But in this strange country, who would be able to tell? She gave her head a little shake, then gathering up her purse and the letter to Kate she made her way to the lobby.

Though dismal and almost spooky the night before, in the daylight it was a cheerful and active place. A large pile of luggage, obviously belonging to departing guests, stood near the front doorway waiting to be loaded on a bus drawn up to the sidewalk.

Several new guests had also just arrived and were checking in at the desk where Megan had registered the night before. She got in line behind them. The clerk had told her she would have her passport back that morning and she knew she would feel safer when it was again in her possession.

Although there was a different man on duty, the word must have been passed for he spoke to her by name. "Ah, Miss More! Good morning! You have come for your passport, yes?" Wherewith, he dived under the desk and produced it with a little flourish. "Your father, I believe, has already gone out. But you, too, will be doing some sight-seeing?"

For all of his pleasantness, Megan didn't care for the question. What difference should it make to him if she went sight-seeing or not? *Unless it would give the girl with the red gold braids who might be a spy more time to snoop around their rooms.*

"I haven't decided yet what I'm going to do." Her tone was stiff. "I would, however, like a stamp. An airmail stamp, for London.''

"An airmail stamp for London.'' He turned, twirled the knob on the safe where Megan's passport had been deposited the night before, took out a box from which he carefully detached a single ·stamp from a large colorful block. However, instead of giving it to Megan he delicately stuck out the tip of his tongue, as quick and darting as the tongue of a snake, gave it a lick and affixed it to the letter Megan had taken from her purse and placed on the counter between them. His hand still covered the letter as he said, "You may leave it here at the desk. I shall be most happy to see that it is mailed."

"*I* will mail it," Megan said a bit too loudly. "I have decided that I shall be going sight-seeing after all."

Before the clerk could do a thing about it—in all fairness she could not be sure that to do *anything* was his intent—she had slipped the letter from under his fingers and into her purse.

After that, she had no choice but to go outside. This she did, and with the clerk's eyes following her—rather balefully, she thought—stepped along in the wake of a large woman wearing English tweeds, sturdy walking shoes and a determined expression.

She continued in this fashion for several blocks to give herself time to think. Maybe the hotel clerk had only intended to be helpful when he said he would mail her letter to Kate. If so, he'd overdone it. Actually, that was what had made her snatch it away from him. He seemed too eager to be helpful. And if she was right in that assumption her letter, instead of leaving Budapest on the next plane for London, would have been steamed open and read, then passed along to the Secret Police or to whoever was in charge of sending what her father called "high-handed telegrams." When she explained to her father her reason for leaving the hotel he was sure to understand.

The baffling part was that anyone should be interested in that letter! There could be no denying that her trip from London had been "programmed" every inch of the way. Step by step, she reviewed it. The boy's presence in London, outside the Cades' apartment. His reappearance in the Frankfurt airport. Even the stewardess on the flight from Frankfurt to Budapest who said "You are American?" had been expecting her. And how neatly she had fallen into the trap, saying, "Why, yes. Does being an American really show?"

The only person not properly briefed had been the officious young soldier she'd dealt with at the airport and that snaffle had dissolved immediately when the older officer arrived, returned her visa and passport and passed her through.

What she minded most, however—her face burned with embarrassment even to think about it—was that she, too, had been "programmed." Like the silly, giddy thing she was—and that was what "they" were counting on her to be—she had allowed herself to be picked up by a strange boy and transported like a bag of flour to the hotel. Worse, when the great flash of lightning split the sky and the terrible clap of thunder had rocked the *kis*, she had felt romantic about him! She'd *liked* having his arm tight around her. Up to the very minute when her father, staring at her in disbelief, had said "I didn't know you were coming," she had wanted to see that boy again. Now, she *never* wanted to see him again.

When a street light turned red she stopped automatically, feeling a little foolish because she'd been so wrapped up in her thoughts she had paid no attention at all to where she was going. At some point she'd lost the stalwart woman in tweeds, but there were plenty of other people milling about on the wide sidewalks. All of them seemed happy, were comfortably dressed and looked well-fed. Indeed, a good many of them were eating little cakes or cookies as they strolled. Even the plump, rosy-cheeked babies—and there seemed to be babies everywhere she looked—were either sucking or munching a hard crusty roll or waving one about. There were also a number of dogs of every shape, size and description trotting along on their leashes or tucked comfortably under someone's arm. A small black dog with a face like a fox was draped around his mistress's neck like a fur piece. Not a hair of him moved except about the last quarter inch of his plumy tail that hung down over the girl's left shoulder.

Suddenly, Megan felt like laughing. What was responsible for this change of feeling? Was it the people? The fat babies? The dogs? Or perhaps it was the auto traffic moving rather leisurely along the wide boulevard (so different from the way cars either raced like a pack of rats down Park Avenue at fifty miles an hour, or else were packed together like lemmings on the side streets where they scarcely moved at all). Or was it simply the blue sky and the warmth of the June sun? Whether one or another or a combination of all ingredients was responsible, suddenly all the little fears that had been accumulating—even the words "Iron Curtain" sounded inflammatory and overdramatic—seemed a little foolish.

Although she'd not kept track of how many blocks she'd traversed, she wasn't worried. Having kept to the same side of the street all the way, all she need do was turn around and retrace the same route to reach the hotel.

At the moment, however, the lovely aroma of freshly baked pastry was drawing her onward as inevitably as the music of the Pied Piper had drawn the children of Hamelin. She might have carried the comparison further, recalling that those children vanished, but the window of the bakery did not allow her to. Never before had she seen so many different kinds of deliciousness! Little pastry pockets, oozing with jams. Cakes glistening with chocolate and filled with cream. Cookies that would have melted whole in the mouth with a single swallow, cookies with icing or sprinkled with nuts, filled cookies and rolled cookies, golden brown doughnuts, fruit pies, soft pies and nut pies, apple tarts, cherry tarts, pineapple tarts, cheese tarts, tarts right side up and upside down! Crepes, flans, babas and éclairs, lady fingers and cakes. One with a burnt-sugar top simply had to be the *dobostorta* that Mr. Dozsás had so mouth-wateringly described.

Megan opened the door and went inside. The place was full. Some people were choosing ,buying or putting goodies all carefully wrapped in paper in the bags made of string that almost every woman she saw seemed to carry. Others were devouring their purchases on the spot, licking their fingers, even licking the last bit of whipped cream from the paper in which the pastry had been wrapped.

Megan made her purchases by the simple expedient of pointing to what she wanted, then indicating with her fingers how many. When all had been transferred to a sheet of white paper which was then folded over and tied with a bit of twine, she was given a scrap of paper with a number on it which she couldn't read. She took it to a cashier near the door who took from her outstretched palm what Megan assumed to be the correct number of *forints*. At least, a half dozen or so ladies who had been interestedly observing her ever since she entered the shop nodded and chattered approvingly. Several of them waved as she departed.

She would have liked to get into her packet of goodies then and there but, as they were all on the gooey side, restrained herself and moved off down the street pausing to look in this window or that. She had stopped again, this time before a display of women's and girls' clothes, all quite nice, when she shivered, quite unaccountably. The sun was still shining and the mood of the crowd on the street was holidaylike. If Kate had been there to see her put on the sweater she'd been carrying, she would have looked at Megan from behind her granny glasses and said seriously that a ghost was walking on the grave of one of her ancestors.

Why Kate said things like that Megan didn't

know, unless it was to see her shiver all over again—which she usually did though she wasn't superstitious. In any case, the thought was enough to make her turn back to the hotel though, for a change, she decided to cross and walk back on the other side of the street.

When the traffic light changed, she streamed across with a lot of other people and began walking rather more briskly than before. By the end of the first block, however, she was almost running. She had not needed to turn to know—though how she knew she could not have said—that someone was following her.

Although the light at the next intersection turned red a second after she had started across, she would not have turned back had not a heavy truck, spewing black fumes, threatened to flatten her.

Even then, it was not an even choice for a hand had grabbed and was tightening on her arm, and a familiar voice was saying—in fact, rather desperately—"Will you, for God's sake, stop *running*? There's a policeman watching."

"I don't care," Megan hissed back. "Get your hand off my arm."

"Only if you promise to . . . well, not to run."

"I'm not going to promise anything."

"You don't need to promise." The boy's voice was as unyielding as her own. "Just use your head."

Although he didn't take his hand away from her arm, he had at least stopped clenching it and when the light turned green again they crossed together as chummily—why did the comparison flash through her mind?—as if they were engaged to be married.

"I'm sorry if I hurt your arm, though you really made me do it. All I really want is to *talk* to you."

"All I really want is *not* to talk to you."

"Then you needn't worry. I'll do the talking," he said, and before Megan realized what he was doing he'd flagged down one of the little taxicabs they'd ridden in the night before and was hustling her inside. Even then, however, she allowed herself only the briefest of glances. No brown raincoat, of course, on this sunny day. His shirt was blue, of some kind of homespunnish material. Two of the buttons were open at the throat with a darker blue kerchief tucked inside. His face was more deeply tanned than she remembered and his dark tousled hair was already burnished by the sun. His hands, too, one of which was planted firmly on each knee, were nice. Not too big, but square and rather shallow with fine gold hairs growing in a patch in the center of the square. The fingers were long, the nails like her father's. Large and oval-shaped, with enough room on them to draw a smiling face.

She made herself stop looking at his hands and turned her gaze outside the window. All the while they'd been talking—or rather, not talking—the cab had been climbing upward but making its ascent so gradually she hadn't noticed that they were really on the heights of the city. The river lay far below, curving gently, crossed and crisscrossed by so many bridges she hadn't time to count them. Steamers, glistening white in the sunshine, moved as slowly as toys pushed by some invisible hand, upstream and down. Above the river the city rose in tiers like the walls of a shallow cup.

András spoke to the driver who paused on a promontory that seemed to drop away almost directly beneath their feet. There András paid the driver and waved him on.

"Come." András took Megan's hand and they clambered down a grassy but rather steep slope. "Here, I think, is a good place to sit. We can be alone to talk." After looking about him as if to be sure this was the case, he turned to Megan almost apologetically. "This is what I wanted you to see. The view from the hills of Buda."

He spoke so softly, almost tenderly, that when Megan looked out where he seemed to be looking, across a soft, rather vaporous void with a lot of blue sky above, she seemed to catch his feeling.

"From here you see what once all the world came to see. The Danube bridges which join our Buda to her sister city, Pest. And there's the Parliament Building, Margaret Island, Fishermen's Bastion, the Coronation Church . . ." A most unboylike sigh seemed to shiver through him. "There cannot be a lovelier sight anywhere than this."

Suddenly, something inside Megan seemed to snap. All the Thomas More stubbornness that had been pent up inside her quietly, but effectively, exploded. "I've seen many sights more beautiful." She got up, twitching bits of dried grass from her skirt. "And the first one that comes to mind is the Statue of Liberty standing in the harbor of New York City. The water may be polluted, you may get mugged if you go twenty-five feet outside your door at night, but it's still a *free* country and I'll take it to . . . to this." She swung her arm around in a giant circle, one that was meant to take in Buda, Pest, the Danube, buildings, houses, everything. Instead, her arm wound up being held rather tightly, almost painfully, behind her back in such a fashion that she dared not move.

"Let me go!"

"Of course. I am sorry."

However, a rather long minute or two elapsed before he did let her go and all that time her face was so close to his she could see her reflection in the iris of his bright blue eyes and smell the clean boy fragrance, a mingling of soap, shaving lotion and toothpaste.

"I'm sorry," he said again, this time meaning it.

She should have been furious with him, but he looked so uncomfortable and contrite that enough anger oozed from her that she could manage a grudging, "That's all right."

The boy's eyes flashed in gratitude, then his expression became sober. "I really did not bring you here to talk about the beauties of Budapest. I thought only . . . that perhaps . . . in these surroundings you would be better able to understand . . ."

"I'd be better able to understand," Megan said tartly, "if you'd simply explain what you were doing following me around London, lurking around in the Frankfurt airport, then last night *pretending* to come to my rescue. And what about that phone call to my father?" She could feel herself getting angry again. "I don't think you made any phone call. You brought me to the hotel because you knew my father wasn't going to meet me, and the reason he wasn't going to meet me was because he didn't know that I was coming!"

The fact that the boy continued to stand, eyes downcast, wincing with every word served not to shut her up but to drive her on. A bad mistake, for now tears were pressing against her eyelids. "What makes it so . . . so despicable . . . what makes it unbearable . . . is that I'd started to like you."

Well, there it was. And with it all out of her system, she started clambering up the grassy slope to the road above.

She hadn't gone two feet before he caught her, sat her down on a grassy hummock and for the second time in less than twenty-four hours gave her a freshly ironed handkerchief.

He regarded her gravely as she wiped her eyes and returned it. "Now could I perhaps talk?"

"I guess." Her tone was ungracious and she looked away from him and off down the river.

"You are too young to have had a job, is that not so?"

She turned to look at him because it was not what she'd been expecting him to say. "Not a real one. Baby-sitting . . ." It was not her fault she'd not had a real job and she resented his asking.

"But you know that people must work?"

"Of course!" If he was trying to irritate her he was succeeding very well.

"Then you must believe that—to use your words—if I was following you around London, observing you in Frankfurt, playing games with you in the Budapest airport and at the hotel, I did it because it is my job.''

''I would not have such a job. I would get a job of a different, a respectable, kind.''

Megan was sorry she'd spoken as she did even before the dark red flush began spreading upward from the open throat of his blue shirt until his face was suffused with it. ''I guess, then,'' he began stiffly, ''there is no point in trying to explain further.''

''At least you could try . . .''

The boy picked up Megan's left hand which lay on the bit of grass between them and looked at it, she thought, as if it were some kind of artifact dug up from some ancient civilization. Idly, he twirled the ring on her fourth finger. ''An opal, is it not?''

''Yes.'' Her tone was defensive. ''It's a child's ring. My father gave it to me on my tenth birthday. Twice, it's had to be made bigger to fit me. But I like it. It . . . it's my favorite thing.''

András made no answer, but stroked her fingers one by one, then returned her hand to the place he'd found it without, it seemed to her, any particular regret.

''What I was saying . . . what I've been trying to say, apparently with little success, is that I am an employee of the State. The People's Democracy of Hungary. Because I am an employee of the State, I do what I am told. It is wise to do so.'' His smile was unsuccessful. ''Any loyal citizen will tell you that. You know what I was told to do. What you do not know is how little appetite I had for the job. I found the idea of it distasteful even before I had seen your passport picture which does not do you justice. Later, after I had seen you—the first time was the day you and your friend rode all over London in a bus—I did not see how I could carry through. But because of certain . . . considerations, I overcame my aversion. I was glad only that I did not know why—and I still do not know why—I was asked to oversee the bringing of a young girl halfway across Europe under the false impression that her father had sent for her to come."

His smile was tight, without merriment. "That is all I really have to say, except to ask you and your father to be careful, please. And to ask that you and your father plan to leave Hungary as quickly as possible."

His expression was so grave, his tone of voice so serious, Megan felt the inside of her mouth grow dry. "Careful . . . of what?"

"I would tell you if I knew. It is very complicated. There are powerful people in Hungary. In Russia, there are more powerful people still. They play games for very high stakes, for which each makes his own rules. I really can say no more."

"But Dr. Dozsás," Megan began, "is he one to be afraid of?"

Instead of answering—there'd been such finality in his voice, she hadn't expected him to—András had leaped to his feet, then bounded into the air in a sort of effortless grand jeté, then returned to earth beside her with something carefully cupped within his hands. Slowly, he opened them just wide enough for her to see a small, copper-colored butterfly resting, wings folded, on his palm.

"A *Lycaena phlaeas*!" Megan leaned closer to study the veinings of the delicate wings.

András gave her a look of pleased bewilderment. "But how could you possibly know? It is a *Lycaena phlaeas*, of course."

"My mother is a lepidopterist," said Megan. She was beginning to enjoy herself, after all. "My mother believes, for instance, that if a child can learn a nonsense rhyme like 'Higgledy, piggledy, my black hen,' she can learn the proper names of butterflies and flowers. I can give you the botanical name of every wild flower, and almost every weed, that grows in the state of Maine."

"Your father is a scientist, also. I know that," András said. "And an inventor. But his most famous invention, I do not know about." Intent on the butterfly, which was now slowly raising and lowering its wings as if to test them before soaring away, András spoke softly, almost idly.

"It is more of a discovery than an invention. And I don't understand it at all, myself."

András smiled as the small copper butterfly, with a slow lifting of its wings, fluttered from his hand, then rising on a current of air floated away. "I dare say, I shouldn't understand his discovery either. Like your mother, I'm going to specialize in butterflies—when the time comes."

Time! Megan had forgotten all about it! She jumped to her feet in a state of panic. "My father! I wasn't supposed to leave the hotel, and he's meeting me there at twelve! It's already now a quarter past."

"You'd better hurry." András took her hand and, scrambling on ahead, half pulled her up the bank to the roadway. "A cab will come soon. All day they come this way after taking visitors to the Heights to see the great sculpture commemorating the liberation of our country."

Scarcely had he finished speaking when a little *kis* came careening toward them. András hailed it, and as he helped Megan inside his face was grave. "Tell no one other than your father that you have seen me. You understand?"

András waited until Megan said "I understand," then thrust a handful of *forints* into the driver's hand. "Hotel Metropole. And hurry."

Megan turned to look out of the window as the cab took off but András had already disappeared.

5
Blackout

ALTHOUGH NO ONE WAS KILLED, the accident was serious enough to tie up traffic ahead of the *kis* in which Megan was riding for twenty anxious minutes.

Amidst much tootling of horns, a crowd was already gathering. Police came, followed by an ambulance. But not until a wrecker arrived and hauled the damaged cars from the intersection was Megan's cab able to proceed. It was all very nervous-making. And her father, of course, would not only be furious because she had left the hotel against his wishes, but he would be thoroughly frightened as well.

She could not blame him. But after waiting so long for her to get back to the hotel, why did he not answer the door? She knocked again, a little impatiently.

Olka, the chambermaid, her red gold hair

glowing and a bunch of keys dangling from a chain at her waist, paused on her way down the hall.

Perhaps, Megan reflected, Olka was a spy. Perhaps, she did understand English as the strange little waiter said she did. In either case, she also understood without a word spoken when someone wanted a door to open. Megan watched as the girl chose a key and slipped it into the lock, turned it, then hurried away.

Before the door was fully open, Megan was yoo-hooing "Daddy!" She stepped into the room. "I'm back," she called. "I hope you didn't worry. I went out just to mail a letter, but . . ."

She was speaking to silence. Even before she checked the bedroom and the bathroom she knew he was not there. The thought that he might be out looking for her only faintly crossed her mind, for in that case he would have left a note somewhere, propped up in plain sight, and there was none. She could only assume that the morning session of the conference had lasted longer than he expected.

In any case, there was plenty of time to take a bath—there was no shower, but only a rather remarkable device that sprayed water in every direction except in the one she wanted—and to put on the best dress she'd brought with her, a navy linen with a huge white collar and a red tie.

She finished both operations, then, to pass the time, settled down at the desk to write Kate the second installment of her Budapest adventure. She would not even try to mail this letter but would give it, along with the first one which was still in her purse, to Kate when she got back to London.

Or perhaps, she would just *tell* Kate what happened and keep the letters as a kind of diary. Or it might even make a book. She could see the words in a headline TEENAGER WRITES BEST SELLER as clearly as if it had been in print. Not that she needed a diary or a book to remember András who, if he had not practically kidnapped her, was most high-handed in the way he had flagged down a taxi, hustled her inside and taken her off to the Heights of Budapest to study the view. And she'd always remember the way he'd looked when he stroked her fingers and turned the opal ring so its colors would catch the light. Most revealing of all was that he had studied her passport picture— though where and how he'd got it was still a mystery—enough to realize that it was *not* a good likeness. Horrible, in fact.

So carried away was she in remembering these and other aspects of the morning it was not until hunger reminded her that she thought of the little pastries she'd purchased that morning. Where had she left them? In the first taxi into which András had plunged her? On the grass where they had sat talking? Or were they still riding around in the back seat of the taxi that had brought her back to the hotel? Wherever they were, they were gone forever and all thought of them vanished as she looked at her watch. Two o'clock and no father. The meeting could not have lasted so late. And if it had, or if there had been an accident or he'd made other plans, she would have had some word. Feeling like a cross parent, she got up and began prowling around the two rooms of the suite, occasionally pausing to look out of the window from which she had a clear view of the street. Taxis arrived from time to time but her father was never in them. A big gray Mercedes pulled into the curb, then backed into a place that seemed to be reserved for it. At least, she'd noticed it there several times before and it bore what she was sure were Russian license plates. As she watched, a liveried chauffeur emerged, lighted a cigarette and, as he smoked, rubbed invisible blemishes from one of the shining fenders with his handkerchief.

Suddenly the act, so simple in itself, the car, the chauffeur, her father's unexplained absence, all seemed so sinister that without knowing in advance that she was going to do so, she crossed the room to the telephone.

"Would you ring the American Consulate for me, please." Her voice was as firm as the resolve, just come to her, that she would not stay in that room another minute without taking some action.

"Excuse, please." The operator's voice was accented but easily understandable. "You wish to call . . ."

"The American Consulate."

"Oh. Yes. One moment, please." There was so much crackling on the line that Megan was forced to hold the receiver several inches away from her ear until it quieted.

"Madame, you are there?"

"Yes."

"I regret that the line is occupied. You will try again?"

"I prefer to wait."

"Madame will wait."

The receiver grew greasy in her right hand and

Megan transferred it to the other then back again before the operator said, "You may go ahead. I have your party on the line."

"American Consulate."

Megan felt tears come to her eyes. If the words had not sounded so beautiful—so *American*—how much easier it would have been to explain why she was worried. And because it had to be done guardedly in case someone should be listening in—she was almost certain she had heard a click on the line—she was afraid it had all come out in a most dreadful mishmash.

In any case, the detached voice found it necessary to ask questions.

"First, will you repeat your name, please."

"Megan More."

"Your father's name?"

"Thomas More."

"It is now three-fifteen. And you say your father has been missing since noon. My dear, that is only three hours."

"It depends on how you count the time." Her mouth was so dry inside she could hardly talk. "He's only been missing since noon if you count the time since he said he'd meet me here at the hotel. But if you count the time since I saw him last, he's been missing since nine o'clock this morning which I don't care for at all!" Megan was aware that her voice had risen childishly at the end but she couldn't help it, and it did seem to have the effect of humanizing the voice at the other end of the line.

"I understand your concern, but I honestly don't think you have any cause for worry.

Perhaps your father is getting out of a taxi in front of your hotel right now. There are any number of reasons why your father could be late returning to the hotel. Have you been in your room all day so that you could have received a call?''

"No, but . . . I was gone for just a little while. I met . . ." Remembering just in time András' caution that she must tell no one other than her father that they had been together, she paused to rearrange her sentence. "I mean, if my father *had* called while I was away he would have left a message with the clerk at the desk."

"My dear child . . ." This was accompanied by quite a human chuckle. "I have stayed in dozens of hotels in cities all over the world, and if all the messages that were left for me and never delivered were placed end to end, they would reach from here to Novosibiriskyie. If you haven't heard from your father by five this afternoon, call me. And in the meantime why not remain in your room at the hotel. And try not to worry."

"I'll try." It was the best she could promise and, indeed, she was already beginning to feel reassured enough to be hungry.

Again picking up the phone, she called room service and ordered a chicken sandwich and a glass of milk. She hoped it would not be brought by the weasel-faced man who had brought their breakfast. But she was not to be that lucky. A little later when a tap came at the door it was he who was standing there, a large tray poised on the palm of one hand.

Making small apologetic sounds, he came slithering in.

Megan indicated the desk which she had already cleared of her writing things. "It will be fine right here."

With a linen napkin the size of a small tablecloth and more apologies, he whisked away a few invisible grains of dust from the desk and laid upon it a fresh napkin and enough silverware for a full meal. Then came another napkin and lastly a small platter covered by a silver dome. The latter he removed with a flourish.

The sandwich, Megan thought, really looked good. The bread was thinly sliced and there were many layers of chicken sliced razor thin inside. There were also the usual pickles and parsley found on sandwich platters in good hotels everywhere. In fact, everything was before her except the milk which still remained on the tray in a bowl of crushed ice.

She signed the check, putting her initials beneath her father's name, then added what she thought was an adequate tip before pointing out that the milk was still on the tray.

The little waiter gave it a nervous glance. "The milk? Oh, yes. The milk. I fear it may not be fresh. Indeed, it may have already spoiled."

"Then why did you bring it? Why didn't you bring me fresh milk?" She knew she sounded like an ugly American, but the fact was that never had milk looked so delicious, so icy cold, with the most delicate of bubbles still on top. She sighed. "O.K. Take it back with you, then please bring me some milk I can drink. I'll call the kitchen and tell them."

The waiter's hand was surprisingly strong on

67

her wrist as she reached for the phone.

"I don't think I would do that," he said softly. "I think today in the kitchen there may be nothing but milk that is, well . . . not fresh." His face was very close to hers. "You do see now, do you not?"

Megan's "yes" was uncertain.

"You will eat your sandwich. It is good. But the milk you will not drink. It is because I am your friend, I tell you this. You understand?"

As Megan nodded uncertainly, he leaned across the desk, made a nice adjustment of the silver, then swiftly as a weasel slipped out of the room.

For a moment Megan looked after him, then walked over and picked up the glass of milk. Even without tasting it, she thought she could detect a queer metallic odor. But she didn't have to be sure of that to know she wasn't going to drink it. Carrying it into the bathroom, she poured it into the basin and rinsed out the glass.

The chicken sandwich also seemed to have taken on a little of the metallic odor, but that had to be imagination and she managed to eat more than half of it before a bellman appeared at the door with a package.

Before she had it in her hand she could tell from a small tear in the paper that it contained the pastries she had bought that morning. Although she'd resisted the temptation to eat one as she walked along, she had not been able to keep from tearing off a corner for a peek inside.

She searched in her purse for *forints*. "A young man with dark eyes and curly hair—he brought the package to the hotel?"

The bellman smiled, then shrugged to show he "had not English."

Megan tipped him. The question was rhetorical. András had to be the one who had brought it. No one else could have known the package was hers.

She carried it into the room, untied the string and inspected the contents. How delicious the little pastries looked! She chose two—a small square made up of many thin layers of chocolate cake with icing in between and a baby éclair almost bursting with a rich filling. It was then she saw the folded piece of paper bearing her name.

Curious as she was, Megan finished the chocolate cake and started on the éclair before unfolding it. Even then, it made no sense at all. Why would anyone be giving her a poorly drawn map? It had to be a map, for the word "Budapest" was marked in red. And the wavy line, running from top to bottom of the paper and looping into a sort of free-form question mark, must be the river Danube, for across the top of the "question mark" were the words "Danube Bend." "Szentendre," "Vác" and "Visegrád" must be towns or cities beside the river, though "Visegrád" seemed to be most important because it, too, was circled in red.

She ate the baby éclair but the longer she stared at the map, the less sense it made. Even the words "MEMORIZE AND DESTROY" printed boldly across the bottom of the map and then underlined struck her as more "cinematic"—she had to grope for the word—than frightening. Perhaps, if she had not been so sleepy. Perhaps, if she had not had to "catch herself" as it were and bring her head up sharply before it dropped to her chest, she would have been able to put together all the little pieces of the plot—"plot," now that *was* a melodramatic word—that had brought her to Hungary. For instance, her father's disappearance (well, he *was* gone, wasn't he?), the strange little waiter and the tarnished milk. "Tarnished" could not be right, but the right word was dancing sleepily beyond her ability to recall.

But to MEMORIZE AND DESTROY. That was the important thing. Lines and letters blurred before her eyes. Although to memorize was impossible, she would pick out something to remember. Visegrád had a pleasant sound. She said it aloud. "Visegrád." And she *could* destroy. She took the little map, folded it in half and tore it. The halves became quarters, the quarters eighths, the eighths the barest snippets. She remembered the gerbil she once had had. The poor little thing had done nothing day after day but sit in the corner of its cage and endlessly tear paper into shreds, looking out from the mound it had made with bright but vacant eyes. Now, like the gerbil, she shredded even the snippets. Carrying them all to the bathroom, she flushed them down the toilet.

She lurched sleepily into the doorjamb, and because her eyelids were so heavy she had almost to feel her way into the bedroom. A little nap was what she needed. But people didn't sleep in the daytime. At least, she didn't. Not when the sun was shining. Something was very queer. In fact, everything was queer. She was so sleepy she did not think she could reach the bed. A little nap . . .

When she awoke, if her father had not returned she would call the American Consulate again. But was not something queer about that, too? The person to whom she had talked had not asked how long either she or her father had been in Hungary, what he was doing there or what his business was. He had not even asked the name of the hotel where they were staying. Such obvious questions to ask, she thought drowsily, unless he already knew the answers . . . Unless she had not been talking to someone at the American Consulate at all . . .

6
"Such a Pretty Little Opal"

MEGAN MOVED UNCERTAINLY. Her head ached and her mouth tasted terrible. Except for a night light burning dimly in one corner she could, at first, see nothing. As her eyes gradually accustomed themselves to the gloom and she made out the outlines of a dresser and a chair, her heart gave a little lurch. *She was not in her room at the hotel*. There had been *two* dressers and *two* chairs in their bedroom there. In this room, the only bed was the one in which she lay. The sheets, however, were fine and soft and the pillow on which her head rested was deep and downy. Next to the bed was a small stand and on the stand a pitcher of what she hoped was water with a glass beside it. As she reached for the latter, a figure she had not seen before rose from the chair, moved swiftly across the room and put a hand firmly down on Megan's own.

"Lie back. I am Natasha, your nurse. You are ill. I am here to help you."

Whether it was the quiet authority in the woman's voice, her monumental size or Megan's own feeling of all-pervading lassitude, she could do nothing but obey. A strong arm raised her head and a straw was placed between her lips.

"Only a sip. More you may have later." She snapped on a light near the head of the bed. "Now it is time for your injection."

As the glass tube of the syringe glinted in the light, Megan sat bolt upright. She had not realized she could muster such strength. "No! I won't! I'm not sick! I don't belong here!"

The nurse, her gray hair drawn back, tightly plaited and bound around her head in a circlet, looked, in her neat blue and white striped uniform, as bland and imperturbable as a female Buddha. She drew back the hand with the syringe, holding it tantalizingly out of reach.

"Oh, we are strong, are we not? Young Americans are very strong! So many vitamins they take. But they are not as strong as the young people of Russia—or the old people either, for that matter. The old people are very tough. They have been through much, endured many things. Now be a good girl and do as I tell you. Shut your eyes and you will feel almost nothing. The medication is only to keep you quiet. To keep you . . . resting until the doctor comes."

As a strong arm pushed her head back against the pillows and the hand with the needle began its descent, Megan again rebounded and with a quick twist of her body half rolled, half scrambled off the bed until she was crouching like a little tiger on the side opposite the nurse. "I won't have an injection of anything! I won't! You have done enough to me already!"

Although Megan had expected the woman to pursue her, instead she suddenly laughed. A deep, belly-shaking laugh that made her eyes disappear in little pockets of flesh. "Very well, then. You shall not have the injection. I like a proud girl. A girl who does not easily give in. The Russian word is *gordyachka*. Now get back into bed and lie quietly and I will tell the doctor when he comes that I have already given you the injection. He will not know the difference." She winked. "If you ask me, he is not a doctor at all but that is not my place to say. But doctor or not, if you get up and go leaping and charging around the room like a wild pony, he will know you have not had it. Otherwise, it is not important. For now there is no use for the drugs. You could not escape from here if you tried."

Megan gave the woman an appraising glance. Though she had laughed, the hypodermic syringe was still in her huge hand.

Docilely, Megan crawled back on the bed. Now that her head was clearing, any contact with the syringe was to be avoided at all cost. "Where is this 'here' that I cannot escape from?"

"Because I am not giving you the injection does not mean that you can ask questions."

"I am not at the hotel."

"No, it is not the hotel where you are."

"Where, then?"

"I cannot tell you."

"Then, how did I get here?"

"You were . . . brought."

"But why?"

"You were ill. The chambermaid . . ."

"Olka?"

"Yes, it was Olka. But why do you ask?"

"I . . . I don't know." Megan shook her head, pretending she didn't remember. But she did. Olka was the one that the funny little waiter had said was a spy.

"Who found you does not matter. But there you were, lying on the floor. When she, this chambermaid, tried to rouse you and could not, she thought you might be dead. Poor girl! So frightened. A doctor is called. He brings you here until you are completely recovered. Health services in Hungary and Russia, all Communist countries, are very good for all the people. For foreign visitors, it is even better. Such as the good care I am giving you. The best. But it should not include conversation. Now lie back at once. If the doctor comes and finds us chattering I will be sent to Siberia."

"To Siberia! You wouldn't. Not really?"

"Perhaps not Siberia, but somewhere else equally unpleasant."

"Dostoevski was sent to Siberia." That fact, unbidden, had simply bubbled up from some deep well in Megan's mind.

The nurse's surprise was genuine. "What do you, a child of Capitalism and Imperialism, know of Dostoevski?"

Megan furrowed her brow in concentration. It still was not easy to put her thoughts together. "A czar—I don't remember which one—sent Dostoevski to Siberia to work in the salt mines because he didn't like what he was writing. But I didn't know that now, I mean . . . that people like you were sent there."

"It is not a proposition I would care to test," the woman said shortly. "Now, no more talking about Siberia."

"It was not *I* who brought up Siberia. I want only to know why I am being kept here. Most of all, I want to know what's happened to my father."

"I told you I cannot discuss it."

"But no one is listening."

"Someone is always listening. Make no mistake of that." The woman looked over her shoulder as if to test the truth of her words. "One more thing. And I tell you this because you are young and foolish. If you would see your father soon, do not try to run away from this place. Instead, do as you are told and when you are told. You are to be kept here in safekeeping until your father decides to do this simple thing. You understand?" The woman picked up the syringe that lay between them on the table, but before Megan could again scramble out of bed, suddenly and with one quick movement injected its contents into a wad of tissue, laughing deeply as she did so. "It is for you and your father I am doing this. Now sleep. It will make the time pass faster."

The floor boards creaked beneath the woman's mountainous weight as she crossed the room. The door was opened, closed and a key turned scratchily in the lock, then all was silence.

Megan lay back against the pillow. Her eyelids were growing heavy again, but she knew she must not give way to sleep. Instead, she must try to put together all that she remembered of the day before. Or was "the day before" still today? A thin whitish line could be seen between the bottom of the drawn shades and the sill but whether it was the light of a new day or the close of an old one she could not tell.

She crept out of bed and knelt at the nearest of the windows. Opened several inches but heavily screened, it looked out from the second floor upon an expanse of carefully tended lawn broken only by the dark surface of a curving drive that appeared to lead to another part of the house out of her range of vision. Little tendrils of mist were rising from the grass. Wisping their way upward, they wove themselves among the branches of the trees, which looked as artfully arranged as the backdrop for a ballet. From their greeny depths birds were calling—not in the sleepy, chittering way they do at nightfall, but in clear glad songs. As she watched, a faint swatch of pearly light appeared. So it must be morning. Morning in the country. But what had happened to yesterday?

How hard it was to think. The funny little waiter who had brought her sandwich and milk was clear enough in her mind. *He* was the one who told her Olka was a spy. *He* was the one who had warned her against the milk and she had thrown it out. But she had eaten half of the chicken sandwich. But had she eaten enough to have drugged her into such a state of insensibility that a whole piece of her life was lost to her forever? Not too likely a possibility, but if not the chicken sandwich, what then? She had eaten nothing else except the little cakes. *The little cakes.* There was something about the little cakes . . . Oh, now she was remembering. András had brought them to the hotel. And she had eaten two, or was it three, of them? Then it was that everything had begun growing dim and that the overpowering desire to sleep had come over her.

Tears of weakness and self-pity slipped down her cheeks and she brushed them away with the backs of her hands as a child does. Could it be that András, who she had thought was her friend, was an enemy? András, who had warned her to be careful and insisted that she and her father must leave Hungary without delay, could he be the one who had drugged her? Was it he who had made it possible for her to be carried away from the hotel like a bag of flour and transported to a house in the country where she was being kept prisoner?

For she was a prisoner. The locked door testified to that. Even if she escaped, how far could she go without her purse which contained both money and passport? She looked down at the wisp of pajama top and panties—which were, at least, her own—with which Natasha, no doubt, had clothed her. But how far could she go in them? For even before she had tugged open the heavy doors of the wardrobe that occupied almost an entire wall of the room and explored its dark recesses, she had known that it would contain nothing of hers. No purse, no suitcase, no navy linen dress with the big white collar and red tie. Nothing but a tangle of hangers, one hanging from the other like the dismembered parts of a Calder mobile.

Megan was still kneeling at the window when she heard the distressed creaking of the floor outside her room. *Natasha*. And this time, the doctor would be with her. Natasha had warned her that when he came she must be in bed and pretend to be asleep. But like Niobe who, weeping beside the stream, had sat so long that she was turned into a weeping willow tree, Megan felt that her feet were rooted in the earth. Already the key was scraping in the lock.

"Please, God, please," Megan whispered. Though she did not quite believe in God, neither did she with certainty *disbelieve* in Him. And it would do no harm. (Kate was the one who was constantly praying like mad for this or that, who claimed that her prayers were answered to a miraculous degree.)

It must have been the prayer that moved her, for a second later she was flying across the room. She had reached the bed, pulled the sheet up to her chin and shut her eyes before the door was opened.

"Poor little thing," said Natasha in a booming whisper. "I cannot help but feel sorry for her. At least, she is sleeping. And while sleeping she does not worry about her father. Perhaps we go away and come back later, yes?"

The reply must have been "no," for footsteps approached the bed and Natasha's voice boomed out again. "Let me wake her then, so she will not be frightened. I still think you do a wrong thing, working through children. There could have been another, a better way to learn the secret the child's father knows."

Through the fringe of her eyelashes, Megan saw Natasha's face looming over her and felt a big, soft hand on her shoulder. "Wake up, little one. Wake. It is the doctor come to see you."

Megan squeezed her eyes so tightly shut that colored lights danced against the black background of her lids, then letting them flutter open, let out a small strangled cry of "No!" and, more frightened than she'd ever been before in her life, threw herself for what comfort she could find against Natasha's huge soft bosom. Then the woman's arms were around her. It was like being locked in the embrace of a giant sofa cushion from which all sight and sound were excluded.

She pushed herself back for air. Natasha was making crooning noises. The fat man standing a few feet away and looking embarrassed was Dr. Dozsás.

Megan was again thinking of taking refuge in the fastnesses of Natasha's bosom, when to her astonishment she found she was no longer afraid. Dr. Dozsás, indeed. He was no doctor, but the Undersecretary in Charge of Foreign Affairs—affairs that were none of his business!

She leaped out of bed, grabbing the top sheet as she went, wrapping it around herself like a toga. "What have you done with my father?"

"My dear child, do not agitate yourself." Dr. Dozsás' voice was creamy. "Your father is in good hands. He is, I hope, at this very moment sharing a symposium—I use the word not in its strictest Platonic sense—with other scientists like himself who are interested in world peace. After his . . . er . . . knowledge is shared, you will be reunited. A special escort, a certain young man, whom you no doubt would like to see again and who is accustomed to dealing with honored guests, will conduct you to the airport where you may enplane for Helsinki which is, I think, your destination.''

"If you think my father will tell you anything he does not want to tell you, you are crazy." She could not keep a note of triumph from her voice. How little they knew her father! "He is . . ." She paused, searching for the right word. "He is incorruptible."

Dr. Dozsás' smile was faint. "My dear, you do not make it easy for me. 'Brutus was an *honorable* man,' if you remember your Shakespeare. 'So are they all, *all* honorable men.' ''

"I'm not so sure about Brutus because I haven't read that play. But I *do* know about Thomas More. He . . ." She let her voice trail away. It was better not to put any new ideas into Dr. Dozsás' head about the way the first Thomas More had met his end.

"Perhaps I phrase it wrong," said Dr. Dozsás. "With your father sharing, it would not be so much a matter of . . . er . . . corruption as of, let us say, establishing priorities. That is, what is most important: for him to share voluntarily with one of the greatest nations in the world a discovery which, in any case, that nation will very soon have discovered for itself, or *not* to share and perhaps allow an unfortunate accident to take place, an accident involving one who is very close to him."

"You wouldn't." Megan spoke with bravery she did not feel. "My father said you wouldn't dare, now that our countries are becoming friends again."

"Who knows what one would or would not dare if circumstances demanded it or certain pressures were brought to bear? Because you do not seem to understand and, even more unfortunately, your father is also lacking in understanding, I shall have to be more explicit. But first, back in bed and pull up the coverlet. Even in June, it is still sometimes chilly in the morning and as the father of daughters myself, I am sensitive to the delicacy of young girls. I would not like our little bird to catch cold."

The remark, apparently meant as a pleasantry, had been accompanied by a smile so terrible, revealing a mouthful of teeth as sharp and pointed as a shark's, that Megan leapt into bed where she drew the covers over her head, as if thus she might escape it.

Dr. Dozsás nodded approvingly. "That is better. Now we can talk sensibly, yes?"

Megan didn't answer but instead concentrated on her feet which were like two chunks of dry ice.

Dr. Dozsás sighed in the manner of one who was only too aware of the vagaries of young girls. "Now, if you will listen, please. I, personally, wish neither you nor your father harm of any kind. It happens to be my misfortune that I have been given orders by someone so important that I dare not refuse. The recent rapprochement—a clever girl like you will have studied French so I need not tell you that it means 'a getting together,' or 'mutual understanding'—between Russia and the United States does not please him. He liked better the power play days before there were such things as cultural exchanges and arms treaties and Soviet and American astronauts playing around together on the moon.''

Again, there came the flash of Dr. Dozsás' shark's teeth. ''Therefore, to have peace in the world, we must have in our possession the most sophisticated method of what we might call 'the search and destruction of aircraft' that now only your country knows. This secret we are now seeking to learn from your father.''

The chill that Megan had first felt only in her feet seemed to have enveloped her entire body in an Arctic coldness.

''You are blackmailing him . . . with me?''

''I would not put it so crudely. I would say, rather, that as time goes by he will become increasingly apprehensive about your welfare. This should make him . . . er . . . more amenable.''

Thinking hard, Megan smiled. She had arrived in Budapest on Tuesday. The better half of Wednesday had been ''lost,'' which made today Thursday.

''There won't be time for you to make my father 'amenable,' even if he chose to be. Tomorrow, Friday, we are flying to Helsinki. He is attending a meeting there and will be staying with a friend of importance. If he does not arrive, even if he should be delayed by as much as a day, there will be people asking about him. *That* could be embarrassing.''

Dr. Dozsás smiled approvingly. ''Very good

logic, my dear. And such would indeed be the case, had we not only yesterday taken the precaution of telegraphing your father's friend—a Dr. Stockmann of the Finnish Institute of Science—expressing his regrets that because of a change of plans he would not be coming to Helsinki as Dr. Stockmann's guest. And your mother, who would ordinarily have the keenest interest in the welfare of her husband and her child is, I understand, incommunicado in the Maine woods. There, I am reliably informed, she is finishing a book on butterflies and moths which promises to be excellent. I shall order a copy for myself as soon as it is available."

Megan dared not raise her eyes. If Dr. Dozsás knew about her father's plans to visit Dr. Stockmann and about her mother's wishing to be undisturbed in the shack in Maine, what else did he know about her? Probably, she thought bitterly, that she'd never smoked pot—though she had on several occasions pretended that she had—that she was poor in math and science and that the family basset, Bernie, a gross, lovable creature weighing sixty-five pounds, was languishing in a kennel in Connecticut.

At that point, Dr. Dozsás picked it up. "I would not worry about the basset. It is generally agreed that most dogs, after a few days, adjust admirably to the family's absence and the kennel in Connecticut is reputed to be very good."

Too frightened and too frustrated to cry, she emitted some bassetlike whimpers over which she could plainly hear Dr. Dozsás clucking like a mother hen.

"There, there, now. It is not so remarkable that I should know such things. The system of surveillance in the U.S.S.R. and Hungary—indeed, in all the East—is very good, though no better I dare say than that employed in your country. But who is not for us is against us—unfortunately, the source of that admirable remark momentarily escapes me—but it is as important to know who are one's friends as to know who are one's enemies." Dr. Dozsás sighed. "Even then, such duplicity exists in man's nature, one seldom can be sure which is which. And nowhere does it evidence itself more fully than in what is called 'love of country.' For 'La Patrie,' 'Der Vaterland,' 'Mother Russia'—it matters not the land of birth —men have killed, betrayed, stolen, lied and cheated. But I am rambling on and such things need not concern you." He smiled, showing his small voracious teeth. "To convince your father that our . . . er . . . negotiations with him are serious and that we, indeed, have you in our . . . er . . . custody, I would like to have from you some small personal possession. Say, your little opal ring? Naturally, after it has served its purpose it will be returned to you."

At mention of the ring, Megan glanced down at her left hand, its fingers so tightly intertwined with those of her right that all feeling had vanished, and quickly thrust it under the covers.

"You *are* making things difficult. But if that is the way you choose . . ." His voice trailed off as Natasha, followed by another woman of even larger size, stepped into the room.

Megan shivered involuntarily. Anything would

be better than to be forcibly restrained and have the ring taken from her. She wiggled it off her finger, thinking of András, who had been the first to notice it, and dropped it into Dr. Dozsás' outstretched palm.

"Such a pretty little opal. It is a pity that some regard it as unlucky." Using thumb and forefinger as a pincer, he regarded it for a moment, then with a quick, deft motion dropped it into the pocket of his coat.

7
The Other Natasha

"AH, BUT YOU MUST EAT!" Natasha cried. "Just look and you shall see how good it is!" She moved the tray closer to Megan, who was sitting hunched on the bed, and held it temptingly a few inches from her quivering nose.

Megan shook her head, though it took every ounce of willpower she possessed to perform the action. Eating was what had got her in trouble before. Eating—and András. For if she had not liked him so much, she would not have let him kidnap her and take her away to the Heights of Budapest. If she had not gone off with him, he would never have got his hands on the little cakes to "doctor" them, thus putting her in the impossible situation in which she now found herself. "Please take the tray away."

Natasha, who had lots of ESP, did not seem perturbed. "I know what you are thinking, but this food I fixed myself. Now there is no need for tricks. See how nourishing and delicious!'' She lifted the lid of a tureen displaying a vegetable broth thick with peas, carrots, meat and tiny egg dumplings. ''And this!'' Off came another lid. ''Paprika chicken with the *nockerl* dumplings! Since coming to this country, though I have not become a serious dumpling scholar—it is said that some in Hungary can tell by the shape of the dumplings who made them and whether the cook was right-handed or left—I would not fear to put my dumplings up against those of the finest chef in the land. Little one, eat. It is important that you do so. We cannot have you looking thin and pale as a little ghost when you go to join your father, which will now be very soon. And this food I know is good for I have fixed it every bite myself.'' Her tone grew coaxing. ''Look, I shall go away and leave you alone to enjoy. See, I am going,'' she added, though she did not go.

Megan felt tears well up in her eyes. ''It's funny, but I guess maybe I do believe you . . . believe that you wouldn't do anything to harm me.'' She managed a small smile. ''The other Natasha tried to poison *herself*. And her mother was good . . . like you.''

''And what do you know of other Natashas and their mothers?'' Deftly, the big woman had placed the tray of food on the bedside table and stepped back several paces. ''Next you will be telling me that you have read the great *War and Peace* and that you are speaking of *that* Natasha.''

''Oh, but I am!'' Megan cried out between mouthfuls of soup and tiny dumplings. ''First, I saw the movie, but I knew the book had to be better so I decided to read it. My friend, Kate, did too."

"But how to read? So many pages." Natasha's look was sly.

"Well, yes. One thousand six hundred and sixty-eight in the two volumes. To read it, we divided each book into halves, fourths, eighths, then sixteenths—and promised each other to read at least fifty pages a day. Most days, of course, we read a lot more than that just because it was so good. One day I couldn't stop. Kate finished it in eight days. I did it in a week—but then I'm a faster reader."

"In Russia, there are many grown men and women, very smart, who have not read it yet," said Natasha dryly. "But the characters? How did you manage to keep track of *them*?"

"Well, we didn't really try," Megan confessed as she polished off a piece of chicken. "We just figured that if a character was really important— ones like Natasha, Prince Andrew, Denisov, Count Rostov and—and, oh, a lot of others—they would keep turning up. And when they did, we remembered them. The unimportant ones, we just forgot. And in the parts describing the battles we may have skipped a little."

Wonderingly, Natasha shook her head, the motion starting little waves of flesh awash around her chins. Then, like a great oceangoing vessel, she turned her great bulk around and sailed from the room.

It was not until Megan had finished the soup, sucked the bones of her chicken, mopped up the last bit of gravy with a final bite of dumpling and begun to sip her tea that she realized something was wrong. No, not wrong. Just different. When Natasha had left the room she had not turned the key in the lock.

Megan felt a strange tightening in the muscles of her chest. Had Natasha merely forgotten? Ever since she'd returned to consciousness in this room, the locking and the unlocking of the door had become so ritualistic that the possibility of Natasha's forgetting seemed unlikely. And if that were so, it could only mean that she had deliberately left the door unlocked.

She got out of bed, tiptoed across the room, grateful that her weight did not make the floor creak as Natasha's did. Happily, too, since she had eaten, she did seem remarkably revived. Not until she reached the door did she notice how pretty the doorknob was. She had never seen one like it. White china with a little spray of flowers painted in the center. Almost mesmerized, she stared at it. Even if the door opened, what good would it do her? Natasha had said she could not escape if she tried. But unless she tried, how would she ever know?

She put out her hand, feeling the knob's cool china smoothness, aware that with the gentle pressure she exerted it was slowly turning. The latch clicked and a moment later she was peering out.

The hallway was big and airy with a window at one end. She could tell it was open, for a breeze was puffing at the thin white material that curtained it. Stepping farther into the hall she could see four other doors, all closed, and stairs carpeted in faded red with a carved handrail, leading down.

She leaned over it, listening. From far, far away in the house she thought she could hear the murmur of voices. More clearly she could hear—probably coming from a room almost directly below where she stood—the sound of someone picking out a faintly familiar melody with one finger on an out-of-tune piano. Making the most noise of all was her heart, which was thumping away like a mad metronome. She gave herself a mental shake. It was nonsense to be frightened. At least she was no longer locked up. And her dress, shoes, purse and suitcase had to be somewhere.

The first two doors she tried were locked and her spirits sank. The third, which was open, must have been Natasha's own, for the closet was filled with tent-sized dresses and shoes which could only have fitted the largest-footed of Cinderella's sisters.

The fourth door opened into a storeroom. A storeroom so full of things that her mind refused to take all of them in. There were dresses, suits, coats and medaled and beribboned uniforms—all of another era and all, at one time, very fine. There were capes and cloaks, caps and bonnets, old-fashioned suitcases—what did they call them? portmanteaus?—boots and shoes, furs and finery of every kind. And in the middle of the largest array of all was her navy dress with the white collar. Her shoes were placed neatly beneath it, and not far away was the little blue suitcase which she hastily opened to find, most miraculously of all, her purse with passport still inside! She kissed the little gray book and in a minute or two had fumbled the linen dress over her head, zipped the zipper and put on her shoes.

In a mirror at the end of the storeroom she surveyed herself. Not exactly the way she ought to look. The navy dress looked as if it had been slept in, as indeed it had, her hair was untidy and her teeth felt as if they were wearing little fur coats. But none of that was important now. Carrying her suitcase, purse still inside, she eased herself out of the storeroom and tiptoed to the head of the stairs.

The murmur of voices could no longer be heard and whoever had been playing that funny little tune with one finger on the piano had gone elsewhere to amuse himself.

A step at a time, she began descending the stairs, careful not to bang the suitcase against the railing. The only plans she had were nebulous. First, of course, to get out of the house unobserved; after that, to find some way to reach the road by some means other than the winding driveway which was in clear sight of the house. The road, once she reached it, would take her either by foot or, if she was lucky, by car to Budapest and the help that only someone at the American Consulate could give.

At the foot of the stairs she paused only long enough to get her bearings. A large parlor, fussily decorated with many little tables and much bric-a-brac, was off to the right. Beyond it lay what looked to be a glass-enclosed morning room into which the sun was streaming. To her left was the library. From the two sides of it she could see, it appeared large, with shelves of leather-bound books from floor to ceiling.

Ahead, a large front hall. A scattering of Oriental rugs, with the rosy muted colorings of stained glass windows, lay on the polished hardwood floor. The door leading outside not only was closed but looked heavy enough to require a strong man to open it.

With this much of the house visible, Megan reasoned that the dining room, kitchen and service areas must lie behind her and that it was from one of these rooms she had earlier heard the murmur of voices. From that direction now, however, came the sound of approaching footsteps. Cut off from the back of the house, with escape impossible from the heavy front door and the library undoubtedly a cul-de-sac, she fled across the hall to the sitting room where, on her way through it, she knocked some small china object off one of the tables to the marquetry floor where it shattered in a thousand pieces.

From the hall, where she had stood but a moment before, Megan heard a man's voice. Though she could only guess that he spoke in Russian, she was reasonably sure that he was angry and that the words were blasphemous.

A second later, Natasha was speaking soothingly in English. "There can be no one there. It is only the cat who has broken something again. I have told you before that you should get rid of him. He is like the bull in the china department."

There was another burst of angry words Megan could not understand, then Natasha's voice came again, still soothing. "Boris, do not be irritated because I speak English and not Russian. It is for practice I do so. And it would do no harm if you would do likewise. As for what is broken, do not upset yourself by looking at all the little pieces. Presently, I will clean it up."

The voices and footsteps retreated and Megan, cowering behind a humpbacked sofa, let out the breath she had unconsciously been holding since the conversation began and tried to make some sense out of it. Two things were certainly clear: that Natasha had *purposefully* left the door of the prison-bedroom unlocked, and that by casting blame on an innocent cat she had managed to keep Boris Whoever-He-Was out of the room in which she was hiding.

Crawling on hands and knees and sliding the little blue suitcase (the culprit, not the cat) ahead of her an inch at a time, Megan managed to make her way from behind the humpbacked sofa, from one place of concealment to another—chairs, draperies, swags of material that covered the many tables—until she reached the morning room. Here, she allowed herself another deep breath and time to take stock of her new surroundings. The room, apparently added sometime after the house was built, consisted mostly of windows. Now, all were open, as well as a pair of French doors that led to a rose garden, bordered by a carefully trimmed yew hedge which was in profuse, almost sensuous bloom.

No one was in sight as Megan stepped out. Crouching down so that the hedge would shield her from the view of anyone inside the house, Megan managed to traverse the length of the rose garden and pass through an archway-trellis affair covered with climbing roses into a fruit and vegetable garden of proportions and variety she would never have been able to imagine.

Cabbages, tomatoes and carrots, red peppers big as bosoms and others small as Christmas tree lights, yellow peppers and green peppers! Green beans, wax beans, baby broccoli, artichokes, brussels sprouts and squashes of every variety. Then came currant bushes, gooseberry bushes and raspberry bushes, all ripe with crimson, rose and yellow fruit—and at the very end of the garden a mulberry bush!

Megan stopped as the name of the little tune she had heard played by one finger on the tuneless piano suddenly came back to her. "Round and round the mulberry bush!"

As she rounded it—surely, that mulberry bush must have been the granddaddy of every mulberry bush in the world—and saw a well-worn path lying ahead, she knew, too, that even that little tune had been a signal from Natasha telling her that she was on the right road to freedom.

As soon as she was out of sight of the house, she began to run. Past a gardening shed—at least, a variety of crude-looking spades, forks, rakes and other implements for tilling the soil were piled in and around it—past a pen filled with fat squawking geese, past a great compost heap and on into a little woods she sped.

Here there was no sound at all except a bird

whose song she did not recognize singing from a branch overhead. But she did not stop running until she had reached the main road. Narrow, but hard-surfaced, it continued on to her left through a grove of trees much like the one she had just come through. To her right, it appeared to lead, after a little way, past fenced-in farmland. After a moment she decided that that road was too open, too dangerous. So she turned left to the road through the trees, hoping it was the right road to Budapest.

Because of a bend in the road she heard the car before she saw it. It was coming slowly, its motor richly thrumming. An *expensive* car. Was it a Mercedes? A *gray* Mercedes with Dr. Dozsás looking out and a liveried chauffeur at the wheel?

Although she had hoped that more time would elapse before her escape from the house was discovered now that she knew Natasha was on her side, she could not take a chance on the oncoming car. In one quick leap, made awkward by her suitcase, she bounded over a roadside ditch filled with turgid water and flung herself down in a smother of weeds and tall grasses. The car was coming closer, still moving slowly, as if looking for someone.

The weeds and grasses were tickling her nose and making her eyes water. If she should sneeze as the car passed her hiding spot, everything would be over.

Even thinking about sneezing sent a message to her brain commanding her nose to do so. But by holding her nostrils shut with the fingers of one hand, and pressing hard on her upper lip with the forefinger of the other, she managed to stifle the explosion as she peered through the weeds and watched the car pass by. Of ancient vintage, it was not gray but black. Not a Mercedes, but of a make she did not recognize. And the driver was a young woman with two small children in the front seat beside her.

Tears of disappointment mingled with the tears caused by the weeds and grasses. She had let pass by a car and driver that would have been the most likely ones to take her safely at least part way to Budapest.

With that opportunity gone she had no choice but to leap back across the little ditch to the road and begin walking. At every step the suitcase grew heavier and heavier. She transferred it from one hand to the other, the arm holding it seeming to lengthen each time by inches.

How many miles she had come or how many miles she had still to travel before reaching Budapest and the office of the American Consulate, she had no way of knowing. Her watch, for lack of winding, had long since ceased to run.

Only one thing remained painfully clear. If the gray Mercedes should now appear, there was no place for her to hide. Woodland had given way to vast stretches of well-tended farmland. Here, even the woods and grasses bordering the road had been cut close and the trunks of the scrubby-looking trees that marched along on either side weren't big enough to conceal a medium-sized girl, to say nothing of her suitcase.

Far off, silhouetted against the blue sky, Megan

saw a combine moving like a great mechanized beetle between flowing, green-growing rows of grain. Closer by were modern-looking farm buildings, painted white. A huge silver cylinder, probably used for the storage of crops, gleamed almost blindingly in the sunlight and reflected itself in a small lake on whose surface sailed what could not have been less than half a thousand ducks and geese. One of the great collective farms, government owned and operated, that she'd read about. It would be unlikely that help for a stranded American could be expected there.

She trudged on. A village that might have been a mirage appeared. It consisted of not more than a dozen or so cottages, each with a primitive device for pumping water—a crude Y-shaped branch propped over a bricked-in well—but with a profusion of sturdy flowers of flaming color in each front yard. In front of one, a woman older than a grandmother, a tattered shawl around her shoulders and her feet bound in rags, was sweeping the street with a crude broom made of twigs and leaves.

Megan leaned her back against the scruffy bark of a nearby tree and closed her eyes.

Later, she was to think that she might even have dropped off to sleep standing up if an approaching horse-drawn cart had not forced her to open her eyes.

Why, seeing it, should she have thought of a *tumbrel* had it not looked so like a drawing in the European history book used at Miss Ivory's School of one of the crude wooden farm wagons used to haul victims to the guillotine during the French Revolution?

Only on *this* cart, sitting high up on the bench-like seat, was a man. Neither old nor young but of middle years, like her father. Also like her father, he had a strong bony face, deep-set dark eyes and the white hair of an older man. Though dressed in the rough clothes of a workingman, there was a dignity about him as he reined in the wretched-looking horse and brought the wagon to a stop beside her.

"Bajban vagy? Segithetek neked?"

Certain that he was offering help even though she did not understand the words the man had spoken, Megan smiled and shook her head. "Budapest," she said, pointing in the direction she had been traveling before she stopped to rest.

"Nem! Nem!" The man cried out in such alarm that for a moment Megan thought she was going to faint, for the man was pointing *his* finger in the opposite direction! She leaned against the tree, grateful for its support, and closed her eyes until the wispy veil of darkness lifted.

The man had already jumped down from the wagon and stowed her suitcase inside. "Buda-pest," he said firmly and pointed once again in the direction he was headed. Then with his two big hands, he hoisted her from the ground to the hub of the wagon wheel, next to the high front seat, and then smiling he lifted a corner of a canvas from the back of the wagon to reveal baskets heaped high with red and green peppers.

A moment later, the man was seated beside her.

He picked up the reins and they began moving off down the section of road she had been walking such a short time before. They passed through the little village and by the great collective farm; through the woods where she had hidden in the grass by the roadside and at last the path she'd followed when she escaped from the house where she'd been held prisoner.

Megan took a deep, reviving breath. Although it had seemed at the time the greatest of calamities that she should have been traveling *away* from Budapest instead of toward it, that accidental wrong-turning now seemed providential. If her absence from the house had been discovered, anyone looking for her would, naturally, have taken the road to Budapest. And not have found her!

The man on the rough plank seat seemed to sense that her spirits had risen for he turned and smiled. *"Amerikai?"*

Megan smiled and nodded. She did not need *The Handy Hungarian Phrase Book* to tell her what *that* word meant, though it did serve to recall something really useful in that little red-bound book. In a minute, she had her suitcase open, extracted the book from her purse and found the page headed "Conversation." Ah, there it was! *"Hol van az amerikai konsulatus?"* she said, plowing into the conglomeration of syllables as if she had been asking "Where is the American Consulate?" all her life.

And, indeed, they must have come out well, for the man, smiling a big smile, said, *"Igen, igen.*

Amerikai konsulatus." Then as new friends do the world over, they exchanged names.

Megan, pointing to her chest, said "Megan."

"Jozsef," replied the man, and he gave the old horse—whose name, he said, was Sacha—a gentle flick with the reins.

8
All On A
Summer's Day

WHETHER IT WAS THE MONOTONY of the road stretching ahead, the rhythmic jogging of the wagon, or the horse's tail keeping time as it swished back and forth in an unsuccessful effort to keep the flies from biting, something was bringing back to Megan's mind bits of a nursery rhyme forgotten since childhood.

"There was an old woman, of whom I've heard tell (joggle joggle, swish, swish), who went to market her eggs to sell. She went to market all on a summer's day and fell asleep on the King's Highway. . . ."

Megan rummaged in her memory for what came next. Something about a peddler by the name of Stout who had "cut the old woman's petticoats round and about." He had cut her petticoats off up to her knees and then had left the poor soul "to shiver and freeze."

Megan frowned. That was not the "point" of the memory. That happened later. Then suddenly she smiled as the lines she wanted returned to her:

> Up woke the little old woman
> And she began to cry,
> "Lack-a-mercy upon me,
> This is none of I."

"None-of-I, none-of-I, none-of-I . . . Now the wagon wheels were repeating the words with every turn and she knew why she had remembered.

"This is none of I," she thought. "This is none of I to whom any of this is happening. It is none of I whose father has vanished, who has been drugged and kidnapped and who is now traveling a back road to Budapest."

She swayed on the seat and her head nodded. Could it be, perhaps, all a dream?

But the sound of a high-powered car approaching from behind was no dream. As if she had been programmed, she slipped from the high seat to the floor of the wagon.

The car slowed down as it passed them, then thundered on down the road.

Slowly, Megan raised her head and peered around the horse's bony flank. It was the gray Mercedes! Or, at least, it was *a* gray Mercedes. The latter thought, however, was little cause for comfort and she again ducked down, her heart battering against her ribs. Crouching there, she glanced up at her companion. If he thought what she was doing odd, he gave no sign. Indeed, from his expression (or lack of expression), one would have thought *he* thought that this was the position all girls from American assumed when a gray Mercedes happened to be passing by.

The thought helped rationality to return. A far more likely possibility, she decided, was that his attention was needed on the section of road on which they were traveling. Apparently under reconstruction, it was filled with chuckholes, small rocks and loose gravel. Dust rose in clouds. Horse and wagon stopped.

Choking, Megan raised her head only to freeze into immobility. Once again, from a distance, she heard the car. Only this time it had reversed itself and was coming *toward* them.

The man, Jozsef, had apparently heard it before she did, for he had already thrown back the corner of the canvas that covered the basket of peppers and tossed her suitcase in beside them. There was no need for him to indicate even with gestures what he wanted her to do. In a second, she had scrambled up onto the seat, then like a child making her first dive into a swimming pool, tumbled headlong into the rear of the wagon and curled herself into fetal position around one of the baskets.

The canvas cover blotted out the sky and the wagon jolted on only to stop again before it could have traveled a hundred yards.

Megan lay without moving, scarcely daring to breathe. She did not need to see the car that had drawn up beside them in a spurt of gravel or hear the scream of brakes to know it was the gray Mercedes. Nor did she need to see the owner of the angry voice. She knew with complete certainty that it belong to Boris who, had it not been for Natasha, would have found her cowering behind the humpbacked sofa in the house in the country only a few hours before.

But if Boris' voice was angry and questioning, that of Jozsef was almost monosyllabic and punctuated only by a few disinterested grunts. With a gift for language she had never before possessed —or, rather, with an extra sensitivity born of danger and necessity—Megan knew that Boris was asking Jozsef if he had seen a girl walking, a girl with a suitcase, and Jozsef was replying *he had seen nobody, nobody at all.*

But if Boris should not believe him . . . If Boris should lift the canvas cover and see her lying there . . .

"Please, God, please . . ." Megan began and, praying and promising, waited until she, at last, heard the Mercedes roar off in a spurt of gravel and felt the wagon start jolting on.

Feeling safe where she was, Megan made no move to emerge, and when Jozsef did not invite her to, she closed her eyes.

When she awoke there was no motion. Not only was the back end of the wagon open to the sky but she had miraculously escaped from the inside of a gigantic pepper where she had dreamed she was being held a prisoner.

Jozsef and another man with a round, ruddy face and a shiny bald head were looking down at her. As both men were smiling, Megan had decided even before the ruddy one bowed and said, "I kiss your hand," that he was Jozsef's friend. Even then, it took a second for her to remember the expression was just a polite form of greeting and Jozsef's friend did not really want to kiss the grimy paw with which she was clutching the side of the wagon.

"Now I lift you down. And while we unload the peppers which Jozsef brings me for my restaurant so my customers may have the best and freshest peppers in all of Budapest, you can use the ladies' room to clean up a little." He winked an eye as round and brown as a ripe olive. "While it is not good for a young lady to travel under canvas with the peppers—Jozsef has already told me of your experience—it is sometimes, shall I say, healthier? Yes?"

"Yes, oh, yes!" Real tears mingled with the pepperish ones as she spoke. "And please tell Jozsef that I thank him. Maybe he even saved my life. I . . . I don't know what would have happened if he had not come along. If there's any way I can repay him . . . anything I can do . . ."

Jozsef had started shaking his head even before his friend had finished telling him what Megan said. Then he replied vehemently at even greater length.

"Jozsef says that it was his pleasure to assist the young American girl and perhaps save her from whatever it was the person in the Mercedes bearing the Russian license plates had in mind. He says, and so do I—though not so anyone can hear—that the Russians who so nobly liberated our country," he paused, cast his eyes heavenward in a gesture of fake piousness, "have now helped us enough and that they should go home to Russia and leave Hungary to the Hungarians."

Megan brushed her eyes with the back of a grimy hand, and managed a little smile.

"Now to follow me to the ladies' rest room, one of the finest in all of Budapest. The gold faucets for hot and cold water are having come from the private bathroom of the former Count Hazyezster when his estate was nationalized."

Jozsef's friend had not exaggerated the glory of the ladies' rest room. The gold faucets, however, did not thrill Megan as much as the hot water that poured from them. She filled the basin, washed her sunburned face and arms, drying them with linen towels as big as crib sheets. She picked bits of dried grass and leaves from her hair, then combed it with an oversized tortoise shell comb she found on a marble table topped by a huge gold-framed mirror. But the girl with the straight black hair and dark blue eyes looking back at her, the girl with the sunburned face and the rumpled linen dress . . . who was she?

"None of I," said Megan faintly. "None of I."

Still, when the girl smiled at her she smiled back because her ordeal would soon be over. Perhaps, when she reached the American Consulate, she would find that her father had already been released and was waiting there to greet her. It was a good thought and she felt almost happy when she trotted out to find Jozsef. At least, when *she* came to write her book, she'd not have to put in those words about the characters "being products of the author's imagination" and "bearing no resemblance to persons living or dead." Kate might not believe her story, but it would be true.

Every word. And best of all it might . . . just might . . . have a happy ending.

The man in the rough work clothing and the girl in the rumpled blue dress attracted no attention, for farm wagons were not an uncommon sight on the streets of Budapest.

When they drew up in front of the building with the American flag flying boldly from its standard, no heads turned as Megan clambered down from the wagon and picked up the little blue suitcase Jozsef had already put down on the sidewalk. They'd said good-bye the best they could a few minutes before—her not small hand almost lost within the grip of his huge strong one—and exchanged words neither understood but whose meaning was clear. Even so, she turned again to wave, then straightened her shoulders and marched toward the flag.

"Your name, please?" The man at the desk was young, assured and full of himself.

"Megan More."

"American?" He smiled as he asked the question, checking the proper square on the sheet before him even before she'd had time to say "yes."

"And your problem? Something lost, I dare say. Passport, suitcase, pocketbook?"

Though the questions seemed flippant, the young man's demeanor and manner of speaking were not. Nor was his attire. In fact, though his accent was strictly Hungarian, he might have stepped out of a Brooks Brothers' window display at the corner of Forty-fourth and Madison in New York City. Still, it was homesick-making and made Megan feel better by the minute.

"*I'm* from New York City," she said, "and what I've lost is my father."

"Your *father*?"

Clearly, it was not the answer the young man had expected and his pen, poised to make another check mark, paused in midair. "You're quite sure *he's* lost—and not you?" His manner had become, if not grave, certainly more interested.

Megan felt a little tide of anger rising within her. "I'm *very* sure. And I'd like to speak to the American Consul himself. It is . . . it may be . . . a . . . well, a national emergency."

"In that case," the young man said, muttering to himself, "it's not the usual thing. Not the usual thing at all." He picked up the phone on his desk, punched a button and after a moment's pause said "Someone to see the Consul, personally." He gave Megan a reflective glance, spoke again into the phone in a voice too low for her to hear, then put down the receiver. "You may wait in there," he said, indicating a door leading into a nearby room. "You should not have to wait too long, though there is another person ahead of you."

Megan again picked up her suitcase and moved numbly off. She had not thought the American Consulate would be like this at all. Although there was a picture of the President of the United States on the wall, somehow she had thought that at every step American flags would come popping up, that legions—well, if not legions, certainly one or two—of uniformed American soldiers would come marching forth to meet her (perhaps with fife and drum) and bear her off to meet the Consul who, like an American Caesar, would set in motion the machinery that would find her father—that is, if he was not already in the Consulate office waiting for her.

Suddenly, her vision blurred with tiredness and worry that things might not be going to turn out right after all. Then an inner door of the reception room opened and panic seized her. All the solid, positive thoughts with which she had been indoctrinating herself swirled away like water going down a drain as two men appeared. One, a man of middle age (afterward, she was to think of him as "the gray man," for his hair, suit, tie and eyes were all of various shades of diplomatic gray, bleaching out to a shirt of the whitest white she had ever seen), had to be the American Consul. The other, plump, egg-shaped and evil—there couldn't be the slightest doubt—was Dr. Dozsás. Obviously, the two were the best of friends for they were shaking hands.

Without thinking twice, Megan turned and ran. For if Dr. Dozsás had told his story first, who would believe hers?

She ran past the young man at the desk who, but a minute or two before, had been counseling her. Ran past the military man at the entrance and down the steps, into the teeming crowd. And into the arms of András.

He swung her around.

She tried to break away, but the effort was useless.

"Walk," he hissed. "This way." And he headed her into a stream of people surging across an intersection. "Did he see you? Dozsás, I mean?"

She tried to show her anger by not replying but András' quiet authority made it impossible. "Dozsás," he repeated. "Did he see you?"

"I don't think so. His back was to me. He was shaking hands with the man in gray."

"I guess that's good," András said. "At least, it gives us a little more time." Eyes straight ahead, András was weaving her through the crowd like a shuttle with a piece of thread. "Dozsás will stay there waiting for you until the place closes."

"But how . . . I don't understand. How could he know I would go there?"

"Where else would he go to find you? That's where I went."

They had turned a corner into a less crowded street. "But how did *you* know?"

András shook his head almost impatiently. "Wait until we can talk quietly. Here's the car."

In spite of everything, Megan was too astonished not to sound amused. If circumstances had been different, she would have laughed aloud.

The car, which was parked on the street and whose door András was politely opening, looked as if it had been put together with spare parts from an automobile graveyard. Fenders did not match and the grill was of uncertain ancestry. Even the hood appeared to have been pounded into shape from a piece of sheet metal.

András read her mind. "Don't laugh. If this car looks as if someone put it together with spare

114

parts from an automobile graveyard, that's because my friend, Gÿorgy, did. We laugh about it because he's a doctor. Anyway, he's lent it to me for, well, for the duration." For the first time since he'd rushed her away from in front of the American Consulate, András smiled. "Moreover, beneath this funny-looking bonnet lurks the engine of a Mercedes 450 FLC."

As they pulled away from the curb Megan could tell that, in spite of its appearance, it was no ordinary car. The steady pulse that came up from the floor was like the beating of a giant heart.

"Although automobiles are not as scarce in Hungary as they were a few years ago, they're still in short supply. Scarcity and expense, however, have made Hungarians the best automobile mechanics in all of Europe. Anyone who is lucky enough to have a car can make it last forever. If he only has a *piece* of a car, he'll find another piece to go with it. Then another one. Until he has a car. Like Gÿorgy. Though not all are quite as original or as good as his."

Suddenly, the disappointment of not getting to tell her story to the American Consul, the near escape from Dr. Dozsás in his outer office, and now having to listen to András—who not only was impenitent at what he had done to her but insisted on going on and on about a wreck of a car about which she could not care less—suddenly, it was all too much. The brave front she had maintained throughout the whole of the nerve-racking day crumbled. She began to cry. Not with tears that slid slowly down the cheeks—like the tears that actresses cry in movies—but with big tears, fat as

115

raindrops, that splattered on her hands and soaked into the navy linen dress. Her wail was as anguished as a child's. "I want my father . . . right now!"

In one impulsive gesture, András' arm was around her, tightening and drawing her closer to him. "Of course. And we shall find him. As for your tears, it is good for you to cry, so you must not be ashamed. All, at times, must cry. Someone has said that man is the only animal that weeps, and it is so."

Whether it was because of the words András spoke, the comfort of his arm drawing her close to him, or simply because her mind was transferred away from the subject of her father to that of her own personal safety, she drew away. For András was guiding the car up an incline as steep and narrow as any street in San Francisco (and more winding) and doing it with one hand.

"You can take your arm away. I . . . I'm all right now. I don't know what it was . . . Something just came over me."

"After what you've been through, you needn't explain," András said. Now both hands were on the wheel and he was backing the hybrid vehicle into a small space between another car and a sight-seeing bus with Russian license plates. "At least, here on Castle Hill I have thought of a place where we can talk in peace. Matthias Church. No one would think to look there."

András hurried her along through happy-looking groups of people who thronged the Heights, talking lightly as he did so. "On warm, sunny days like this everyone who can comes here.

116

It is the oldest part of Budapest. People like to look at St. Stephen sitting there on his horse." András smiled and his dark blue eyes shone. "A wise and great man, he was the first true king of Hungary. And there on your right, looking like an illustration from a fairy tale, is the Fishermen's Bastion. Though it looks old, with all of its arches and turrets, it is modern. During the siege of 1944–1945, this part of the city suffered the most terrible devastation of all. But much has been rebuilt according to the original plans. And some good came out of all the destruction. Under the rubble were found many older walls and arches, some from medieval times. And here . . . here is the church."

As they stepped into the dim interior and slipped into the shadows of a pew, Megan noticed that, except for the lone figure of an old woman praying before an altar backed by a flickering row of votive candles, the church was empty.

"If we talk quietly," András said in a low voice, "we will disturb no one. And I think King Matthias the Just—he came after Stephen by four hundred years—would like to have us here. He is the one who restored the great castle of Visegrád. Like Harun-al-Rashid, not only did he encourage art and learning, but folk tales grew up around him, too. He liked to put on the clothes of a peasant and mingle incognito with his subjects. Unfortunately, his nose was of such magnificent size it made disguise difficult."

In spite of her worry, in spite of everything, Megan laughed.

"That is a good sound to hear. Fear clouds the

mind, makes clear thinking difficult.''

"So does not knowing," Megan said. "I still don't know what happened to me. Or how. Or who was responsible—even if it was . . . you."

"No!" András' reply was so explosive that the old woman at the altar rail turned to look. His voice softened. "Not I. You must believe me."

"How can I? After what you did to the little cakes!"

Having at last put into words the thought that had been tormenting her, she should have felt better. But it wasn't working that way at all. András looked as if he might be having a heart attack.

"I . . . I don't know what you mean. After I'd put you in the taxi I went back to the place where we'd been sitting . . . you and I . . . to think. There I found the package of little cakes. I brought them to the hotel . . . left them with a bellman I know and asked him to take them to your room."

"You didn't . . . do anything to them?"

"For God's sake, no!"

Megan shook her head wordlessly.

"If there was something wrong with the cakes . . . if they were drugged, it happened after I left them at the hotel. I swear to you that. You have to believe me!"

Megan's eyes searched András' face. No one had ever looked less guilty. But still . . . "All I know is that it couldn't have been the milk," she said stubbornly. "The waiter said I should not drink it, so I threw it out."

"This waiter." András had tensed. "What did he look like?"

Megan tried to think back. It seemed a lifetime

ago that she'd seen the little man for the first time. That had been at breakfast . . . could it be only two mornings before? The second time was that same day when he brought the chicken sandwich and milk. "Small," she said, "with sloping shoulders. And a face . . ." She hesitated, it seemed such a dreadful way to describe a friend, "a face like a weasel."

"Laszlo," András said bitterly. "A perfect description of Laszlo Krudy. I should have known Dozsás would have worked him into the hotel somewhere."

"He . . . he's not a waiter?"

"He's anything that Dozsás wants him to be in the dirty tricks department. Waiter, chauffeur, office worker. Wherever there's anything underhanded going on, that's where you'll find Laszlo."

"*You* work for Dozsás, too." Even if András did have a heart attack, she felt she had to say it. "How do I know that what you tell me is the truth?"

"Because I love you."

The words, so simply and so softly spoken, exploded like a firecracker inside Megan's head. The explosion was followed by an equally shattering silence.

"You . . . love me?"

"I don't want it to embarrass you. I don't expect you to love me, even to like me. At least, not after all that's happened. But from the first moment I saw you in London, I haven't had you out of my mind. And, I might add"—András' voice was almost bitter—"ever since then I have been almost out of my mind with worry. That's why I went to your hotel this morning. To find out if you'd gone back to England—or wherever it was you were going—as I'd advised you to do. When I found that instead of checking out you had become 'violently ill' and had been taken away by 'friends,' I was frantic.''

"Love!" thought Megan. Her lips silently repeated the word. Had András said he loved her? It was impossible. She was asleep. She was dreaming. No, she was awake but she was sick. Delirious. Whatever she was, she wanted to hear more. But András was apparently through with his declaration of love and now sat hunched beside her in the pew staring at the knuckles of his clenched hands as if he had never seen them before.

Megan cleared her throat. "Who . . . who told you I'd been taken away by friends? Someone at the hotel desk?"

"No. I wouldn't expect any of the people in Dozsás' camp to tell me the truth about anything. Though I did see a suitcase near the porter's desk that I thought might belong to your father. It was an American make—I've seen them in London—and when I looked, it did have your father's name on the luggage tag. I went looking for Olka. I found her on your floor of the hotel making up beds and she told me. She knows what goes on in all the rooms.''

"But Olka is a spy. The waiter told me that."

"Who is or who is not a spy? And for what? Who is or who is not a friend? Sometimes, it is hard to determine. But I know about Olka. She is bitter against the government. The young scientist to whom she is engaged wants to take further study in Germany. If he goes, he will not be allowed to return. Nor will she be allowed to go with him. It is the brain drain the government fears. Thus they keep people here. For the intellectual, it makes life very hard. Even if the visa for travel outside the country is procured, few have the money to travel on. The *forint* is worth nothing outside Hungary. In any case, it was Olka who told me you were taken away. I borrowed Gyorgy's car and drove to the country home of the Russian, Boris Bolonski, who serves as the eyes of the Kremlin in Budapest. It is he who makes plots with Dr. Dozsás—plots like the one that brought you and your father here. They, with others, hope to depose Janos Kadar, who since 1956 has brought many reforms, and reinforce ties with Moscow from which we long to escape.''

Megan's mind was whirling. Only one thing was clear and that was worry about András' safety. "What if Dr. Dozsás had seen *you* . . ." She shuddered.

"I made certain Dr. Dozsás would not be there when I arrived," said András dryly. "Besides, he thinks I am today on party business in Székesfehérvár.''

"Székes . . . what?''

"Székesfehérvár.'' András repeated the word, laughing. "In Hungary, names of towns and cities are either very long—like Hódmezővásárhely—or very short. Like Pécs or Vác.''

"Vác.'' Megan whispered it to herself. There was another place that András had mentioned a

121

few minutes before. Visegrád. It was still floating like a free balloon in her mind.

"But to go back. I left the car in the woods, took a back way into the house and found Natasha. She told me—not, I thought, too regretfully—that you had escaped. I didn't question her as to how this had happened. I just made for the American Consul's office as fast as I could get there. I knew, too, that the minute Dozsás found you were gone, that was where *he'd* go looking for you. I only hoped you'd get there first. From that point, you know what happened. Now, you're at least free. And we can go about the business of finding your father, though I think, for the time being anyway, we'd better keep the American Consul out of it. Dozsás will already have told him such a story—he is a most persuasive man—he might not believe the story *you* told him."

Occupied by her own thoughts, Megan was only half-listening. "Vác and Visegrád. Aren't they rather close together?"

"Just around the bend from each other on the Danube. Why?"

"The map I was to memorize and destroy."

"What map is that?" András' voice was sharp.

"It was tucked in with the little cakes. I thought it had got in there by mistake at the bakery—though I didn't see how. Or know why."

"What else do you remember about the map?" András was intense.

"If I tried, maybe I could draw it again. I was already getting sleepy when I looked at it, so it's not very clear. But I did tear it in little pieces and flush it down the toilet just before everything went black.''

András had produced a piece of paper and a pencil before Megan could rummage either from her purse. "Here."

Megan scooted over to the entrance of the pew where there was more light and began to draw, furrowing her brow as she did so. "Budapest was at the bottom, I remember. Then there was a kind of wavy line, like this, running from the bottom of the paper to the top where it turned into a kind of question mark. Near the question mark were the words 'Danube Bend,' so I figured the wavy line must be the Danube. Then there were some towns marked. Vác was one. I remembered as soon as you mentioned it a few minutes ago. And Visegrád, too. It was about here." She made a little "x" to mark the approximate place. "I thought it might be important because it was circled in red."

"Visegrád!" András whispered. "Of course! They've taken your father to Matthias' Castle at Visegrád. The one I was telling you about. It's been closed to the public so far this summer because there's been some new excavating and restoration going on. But if Dozsás got rid of all the people working there—they're mostly students and volunteers—your father could be kept there for six months and no one would ever find him."

"But who could know my father was being taken there? Who could have drawn the map and put it in the package with the little cakes?"

"Olka, I suspect. She could have overheard

Dozsás and Boris Bolonski talking while she was making beds. They keep a suite at the Hotel Metropole so they'll have a place to do their plotting. In fact, this morning she was on the point of telling me something more when Laszlo Krudy came weaseling down the hall. I got out of there in a hurry. I didn't want him reporting to Dr. Dozsás that he'd seen me talking to Olka. But where the map came from isn't the important thing right now. There are at least a half dozen people working around the hotel who hate Dozsás because he is a traitor to the country. Any one of them could have found out about your father being kept a prisoner at the palace while they tried to pry something out of him. It is a joke in Budapest that if you tell a secret to a friend it remains as confidential as if you had broadcast it on the radio. But this is no time for joking. As soon as darkness comes, we'll start for Visegrád. If your father's there, we'll have him out of there before morning.''

9
The Castle
Of The Kings

THE MOON HAD RISEN, as András said it would, great and golden. Then, as he predicted, clouds had come. "Wait here," he said. "I shouldn't be too long."

Watching him lope off into the darkness, all of Megan's doubts and anxieties swooped down on her like evil birds of prey. What if András, at this very minute, instead of picking up her father's suitcase which he said he'd seen in the lobby of the hotel that morning, was instead in a telephone booth calling Dr. Dozsás to tell him where she might be found?

She had no such doubts when András was with her. That evening at sundown when, hand in hand, they had climbed the winding stairs to the highest of the turrets of the Fishermen's Bastion and watched the shadows lengthen, the river darken and the lights come on all over the city, she had believed him when he said they would find her father unharmed. She'd almost believed him, too, when earlier he had said he loved her. She was still grateful that he had not asked her to respond. For what would she have said if he had? What did she know of love? Nothing at all. Only that never before had she tingled from head to foot as if an electric current were passing through her body when a boy had touched a forefinger to the faint blue vein inside her wrist. Nor had she ever trembled deep inside as she did when he brushed her long bangs to one side and held them there and looked at her as if he were memorizing every inch and aspect of her face.

Perhaps, just as important, never before had she talked to a boy the way she had to András.

Talked about personal things. She'd told him that when her mother and father met it was "love at first sight" and András had nodded, pleased, because, he said, that was the way it had been with him.

With her parents the cataclysmic event had occurred at an outdoor reception following a wedding. Her father had been best man, feeling silly in morning coat and striped pants. Her mother, whom he'd barely met and to whom he'd spoken only a few words, was a bridesmaid and was dressed in ruffles and lace, which was not her type at all. Nor his. All that changed, though, as she suddenly darted from the receiving line—just as the most honored guest was passing through—and went crashing off, ruffles and all, into a nearby thicket of pink japonica.

"There was this rather nasty silence, sounds of

threshing about—and I'm afraid a few 'damns' and 'hells'—before she came out again. Her bridesmaid's dress was torn, her hair falling down and her bouquet gone forever, but between her thumb and forefinger she had a *Morpho rhetenor*, a moth never seen before in all of North America. Even at a wedding reception, she couldn't resist going after it. And, of course, my father couldn't resist her. They were married within a year and had me nine months later.''

It had not been necessary to tell him *that*—but she had. And she'd told him, too, about the first Thomas More who had married the eldest of three sisters because he was afraid she'd feel bad if he passed her over in favor of a younger sister he much preferred. She'd told him, too, that it was for Thomas More's daughter, Meg, that she'd been named.

And what had András told her? That the palace at Visegrád had 350 rooms and that after the Turks had razed it, earth slid and washed down until the ruins were completely covered up. Not until 1943 had someone digging around discovered them. A very big deal.

Even the little she knew about András she knew from her own experience and that was not completely reassuring. Was she not taking a terrible chance putting her father's safety and her own into his hands?

Time was passing and she shivered in the night air. András had said that unless he could talk to the American Consul himself, it would be useless to report her father missing. But might not András have said that to suit his own purposes?

Perhaps, even now, it was not too late to slip out of the car and try to reach someone at the Consulate.

She had one hand on the car door when in the faint glow of a street light she saw him coming. He was carrying what looked to be a suitcase in one hand and a briefcase in the other.

"Got 'em," said András as he approached the car. "No trouble at all. I told the fellow at the desk that Dr. Dozsás had asked me to pick up the suitcase and briefcase belonging to the American Thomas More. Didn't know if your father had a briefcase or not, but thought I might as well ask. And sure enough, the fellow trotted it out. Even told me the bill had been paid and gave me a receipt. How's that for Hungarian hospitality?"

To Megan it seemed a poor time for joking. "I want to see if it *is* my father's suitcase," she said coolly. "It doesn't matter about the bill."

"Only to the extent that it shows Dr. Dozsás plans to release your father as soon as he tells Dozsás whatever it is he wants to know."

"My father will never tell."

"Hopefully, there will be no need for him to if we get there in time."

András put the suitcase up on the hood of the car and played the beam of a flashlight on it. "Maybe this will help."

On one side of the battered-looking suitcase were the letters TM, formed from yellow adhesive tape. She had put them there herself. The toothmarks on one corner could have been inflicted by none other than Bernie the basset hound, years ago when he was a puppy. "It's his suitcase," she said. And after she'd looked at the almost new Mark Cross case—her mother had given it to her father only the Christmas before—added, "And his briefcase, too." She put it on the seat beside her though it offered no comfort at all. For the first time, the possibility that she might never again see her father alive crossed her mind.

András drove effortlessly, his long-fingered hands scarcely seeming to touch the wheel as they guided the car down the winding highway.

Budapest and the island of Szentendre, built up, András said, by immense deposits of silt and pebbles carried geological ages ago from the Danube's source in the Black Forest, had long since been left behind.

Now, having left the plains, they drove through dark valleys with mountainous masses rising on either side. Or followed the serpentine outline of the Danube glinting like obsidian in the moonlight. Climbing, descending and climbing again, they passed lonely cottages and traveled through sleeping villages.

"We're not far from Visegrád," András said. "Another ten, perhaps fifteen minutes. By then it will be midnight. No one in the village will even be awake."

"What are we going to do when we get there?" Since they had started, Megan had scarcely spoken.

"Park the car somewhere near the landing stage—Visegrád is on the regular steamer route to

Budapest—then reconnoiter. Look for signs that would tell us they've got your father hidden somewhere inside the castle.''

"But I thought we knew for sure that is where he would be . . .'' Megan's voice cracked with nervousness. "I thought the map showed us that.''

"We're not going to know anything for sure until we find him.''

"But when we do?'' She hesitated. She wished she could see András' face so she would have some idea of what he was thinking but no clue was to be found in his dark profile.

Minutes passed before András spoke and even then it was a disappointing "I don't know—except to get you and your father out of the country as fast as possible.''

She had no choice but to keep on asking questions. "But for that, don't we have to have some plan?''

András nodded. "But the plan is going to depend on time. That is, how much time we have before Dozsás discovers that your father's not his prisoner. The quickest way out of the country would be to drive to Komárom—that's about eighty kilometers from where we are now—and cross over into Komárno, on the Czechoslovakian side.''

If only she had learned the metric system when she was supposed to she would not have had to ask how far eighty kilometers was in miles.

If András thought the question stupid, he didn't show it, but said, "Divide by five-eighths, which makes it about fifty miles,'' and went on as if he had not been interrupted. "Crossing into Austria instead of Czechoslovakia might be less risky, but Sopron is a good 140 kilos beyond Komárom. And at any border point—with one road block behind you and another ahead and an armed sentry looking down at you from his turret—you could be held on the smallest technicality until Dr. Dozsás caught up with you. That's why I'm thinking our best bet might be to return to Budapest and get you and your father on the first plane going west. But, of course, no plan is going to work unless . . ."

A hard knot filled Megan's throat. "Unless . . . what?"

"Unless your father still has his passport and Hungarian visa in his possession."

"And if he hasn't?"

"In that case, he's not going anywhere—certainly for a while. But there's no point crossing that bridge until we come to it. Soon we'll know a lot of things. How closely your father is guarded and what I have to do. And to whom."

A shiver went down Megan's spine.

"In the meantime," András continued, "there's no need to announce our arrival." He flipped a switch on the dashboard and in darkness the car crept down the main street of a village where he finally brought it to a stop in the shadow of a small building. There he collected his flashlight and a small bundle from under the seat of the car, stuffing the latter in a pocket of his jacket. "After I leave, lock the doors. You'll be all right until I come back."

"But I'm coming with you!"

Though it had been a cry of anguish, András'
"no" was decisive. "With all the loose stones,
staircases and different levels of the palace, it is
dangerous even for me at night, and I know it
well. As a small boy I explored it inch by inch with
a cousin who lived here then."

"Then after you leave, I shall follow you."

There was a moment's awkward silence, then
András laughed softly. "Well, if you must, I suppose you must. But only part way." Already he
was out of the car, holding his hand out to her.
"But we must keep to the shadows."

The injunction hardly seemed necessary.
Although here and there a light glimmered faintly
from one of the cottages, the only accompaniment
to their silent footsteps was the rustle of leaves in
the branches of the avenue of trees down which
they walked and a chorus of katydids singing all
around them. An owl hooted lonesomely to an
answering mate and a small creature, more
frightened than Megan was, skittered through the
grass at their feet.

When András said, "We turn here and go
through this courtyard," she followed, almost
hypnotized by tiredness. How could a day have
held so much and lasted so long?

It seemed almost as if a spell had been cast over
the village decreeing that its human inhabitants
should sleep until morning came. Indeed, so great
was the feeling of unreality—that she, an
American girl, should be walking at midnight with
a boy down the streets of a village that had once
been a Roman fortress, or that her father should
be held a prisoner in the great, hulking structure

that loomed before them in the light of the pallid moon—that she ceased to be afraid.

Her hand was held so tightly in András' that she stopped when he did.

"In a moment, when the moon comes out from behind that cloud, you can see how great a palace it was with its courtyards, treasure chamber, the hall for the holy crown . . ." For a moment, his voice grew hushed, then once again was practical. "But all those rooms on the upper levels are open to the sky. There would be no way to keep your father hidden while the . . . the negotiations were going on. What you cannot see, below the lowest level of the lower ceremonial courtyard, is a cellar. It stands restored as it stood four hundred years ago. It is there I'll go first. If someone's on guard, I'll know your father is there."

"But the guard . . . How will you get rid of him?" The thought that had just occurred to her was almost too dreadful to speak aloud. "Not . . . not shoot him . . ."

András laughed. "Don't be silly. I don't carry a weapon, ever."

"But how . . ."

A second later, Megan felt a rush of air as András' right hand sliced downward in the darkness not more than an inch away from her nose, accompanied by a most realistic groan of his own manufacture. Then he laughed. "Easy, if you know how."

"But if something goes wrong . . ." Suddenly, her heart had started pounding in a fashion even crazier than before, for András' hands were on her shoulders and his face so close to hers she could feel the warmth of his breath.

"Nothing will go wrong," he whispered. "Nothing will go wrong, I promise you . . . if I may kiss you."

As brief as it was, his lips pressed hers so softly and with such sweet and gentle pressure that the kiss seemed to linger even after he had disappeared in the shadows. Not until a straggling veil of clouds that had covered the moon passed by could she see his crouched figure running only to vanish again.

How many minutes passed, she had no way of knowing. A sharp report came from the direction of the palace. A gunshot—or a falling stone? So intense was her concentration as she peered into the darkness in which now the outline of the palace, in the moon's pale glow, was barely discernible, that she heard the sound of scuffling feet and heavy breathing before she saw the strange, crablike figure moving toward her. No, it was not one figure but two. One was supporting, almost carrying, the other.

She put her hand over her mouth to keep from screaming, then spoke in an anguished whisper. "Daddy? András?"

"I've got him," András answered. "He's all right, I think. The key to the car is in my right-hand jacket pocket. Take it. Start the car and bring it to the entrance of the courtyard. There where we turned. And hurry. If I let your father down I'm afraid I won't be able to get him on his feet again."

She stood for a moment, fighting off an almost

uncontrollable impulse to throw herself at her father's feet, kiss his hands, his face, beseech him to speak to her, then turned and in almost total darkness ran until she reached the main street. There she paused. From which way, right or left, had they come?

Blindly, she turned right and had gone perhaps a hundred yards before some instinct told her it was the wrong direction.

As she retraced her footsteps, her heart pounded in frightened rhythm and did not lessen its beat until she came to the small building in the shadow of which András had parked the car. Even then, the palms of her hands were so slick with perspiration that she twice dropped the key before managing to place it in the ignition lock. Worse, the motor failed to turn over and, afraid of flooding the engine, she forced herself to count to five hundred before trying again. On the next attempt, however, it growled reassuringly, and without further trouble she brought the car to the entrance of the courtyard where András waited, bent almost double from the weight of her father's body which he now, somehow, seemed to be supporting on his shoulders.

"You'll have to help me get him in the car. The back seat will be best. You get in first. Take his shoulders. Try to support his head. I'll do the rest."

She was too frightened to do anything except what András told her. Not until they had managed to wedge, fold and shove her father's not inconsiderable length into the back seat did she have the strength to whimper, "Why doesn't he talk? What have they done to him? What are we going to do now?"

András, still breathing heavily, shook his head. "Talk later. Now we've got to get out of here, back to Budapest and to the airport as fast as we can."

With a quick turn of the wheel and a deft manipulation of the gears, the car shot backward a dozen feet, then roared forward, a dark shape tunneling down the even darker road to Budapest.

Woven into a cocoon of misery, Megan did not stir until András' hand sought hers, holding it tight. "Try not to worry. Your father's going to be all right. His pulse is strong. I made sure of that before I carried him out. And while I had the chance, I checked his passport and visa. Both safe in an inside pocket of his jacket."

As if he understood, though dimly, that he was being talked about, Megan's father began to stir. Her heart quieted. He was going to be all right. She had to believe that. Just as she had to believe that returning to Budapest was the right thing to do. She even managed to compose herself sufficiently to listen to András' account of the rescue.

"Obviously, the fellow on guard wasn't expecting anyone to come. Else he wouldn't have been curled up like a dormouse at the entrance to the cellar snoring his head off. But there he was, so sound asleep he didn't rouse when I stepped on a loose stone and sent it tumbling down the stairs. Luckily it was so dark he couldn't see my face—I'd not like Dr. Dozsás to know I was mixed up in this—so all I had to do was tie his mouth shut and truss him up like a holiday goose.''

"Then you went to look for my father?''

András nodded. "He was asleep, too. Drugged, I should say, lying on a cot with a pillow and a blanket. There was a table, on it a jug of water, the remains of a meal and part of a bottle of wine. Whatever Dr. Dozsás wanted from your father, I guess he thought he'd have better luck if your father had something to eat.''

"Whatever Dr. Dozsás wanted to know, my father wouldn't be influenced by his *stomach*,'' Megan said stiffly. "I do not think he would give away his country's secrets—even for me.''

Until that moment, she had never put the thought into words. What would she have done in her father's place? Would she not have given away her country's secrets—given away anything—for him?

The sudden chill that had spread through her intensified as she felt András tense beside her.

"Is . . . is something wrong?''

"We're being followed. I suspected it a little while ago but until now, when they are trying to overtake us, I couldn't be sure. Turn around and take a look.''

At first, she could see nothing, then as the road turned again, two lights gleaming like cat's eyes appeared in the distance. Even as she looked they came closer.

"But do we know for sure it's one of *them*?''

"Not for sure. But it is for sure that as soon as that fellow I tied up gets himself untied he'll send for Dozsás or Boris. Get either of them, or both, on our trail, and we haven't got a chance. Gÿorgy's car is fast but the Russian's is faster. The only thing we can do . . . is to be smarter." As he spoke, he doused the headlights and the highway that had been spreading like a pale white ribbon before them disappeared. Instead of going forward, they were reversing at almost a right angle to the road. Branches and leaves were brushing the sides of the car. For a moment the back wheels spun helplessly, then regained their grip; the car again moved backward and András turned off the engine. "There's a chance we may never get out of here, but there's a better chance our friends will be traveling so fast they'll think we're still ahead of them and not behind."

Only seconds later, the thunder of the approaching car shook the stillness. "It's a Merce," András said, and his arm tightened around Megan's shoulder as twin swatches of light cut through the night and a dark shape hurtled past. In the faint glow of the taillights, they could see the Russian license plates clearly.

10
Good-Bye
To Budapest

MEGAN DID NOT WAKEN as András pulled
the car into the rutted driveway and out of sight
behind a small one-story house. Nor did she stir
when a few minutes later he and a stocky man with
a bushy reddish gold beard and thinning hair
moved her father from the back seat and
"walked" him into the house.

Returning, András whispered her name and the
word "darling" more softly still. He pushed the
dark straight bangs aside and "drew" her profile
with a forefinger but not until his lips lightly
brushed her cheek did she stir.

"Wake up," he smiled. "We're at Gÿorgy's."

For a moment, Megan stared at him blankly.
Tiredness had so completely overtaken her that his
words did not make sense. Even András' face
looked like a large pale moon in the thin light.
"We . . . we're not at the airport?"

"No. I thought it best to come here first, find out the time the next plane will be leaving for the West and have Gÿorgy check your father and see if he's O.K. to travel. He's doing that now while Olka fixes breakfast. She has to be at work at the hotel by six."

"Olka?"

"I guess I didn't tell you. She's Gÿorgy's sister. This is their house. They live here with their mother and a married brother and his wife."

Megan shook her head as if the motion might brush away the cobwebs that obscured her mind. Olka was a spy. No. She wasn't a spy. It was the waiter with the face like a weasel who was the spy. Olka was Gÿorgy's sister. They were good.

András held out his hand. "Come," he said.

Like a sleepwalker, she went with him through the back door of the house into the kitchen.

Long afterward, the scene was still imprinted on her mind as clearly (and in color) as if fixed on sensitized film. A kitchen so small the table with the red and white checked tablecloth almost filled it. Steam geysering from the spout of a teakettle that sat next to a huge pot of porridge exploding with miniature craters. Olka, her burnished hair shining in the glare of an unshaded overhead light bulb, was standing with her back to them as she spooned batter onto a sizzling cast iron griddle. She turned when András spoke her name.

"Olka, I think you and Megan have met before."

Olka wiped a hand on her apron and extended it to Megan. "We meet, but we do not talk." Her bright blue eyes were impish. "It is better if people at the hotel think I am a dummy and do not know English. Besides, it is not necessary that I talk to her to tell her what I know. That while I am making up beds, I hear Dr. Dozsás and the Russian, Boris, talking in the next room. They decide where they are hiding your father. Right away, I draw the little map. Then I see my friend Míklos, the bellman, delivering the small package to your door. He lets me put the map inside.''

''That solves the mystery of the map,'' András said, ''though I told Megan I thought it had come from you.''

''But I worry, though, you not find it in time. Already I am learning from another friend who works in the kitchen that something funny there is happening to the food going to your room. Later, when I find you fainted, I *know*. But now you must eat before your journey.''

Megan brushed her hand across her forehead, but in the steaming kitchen with its bright light and smell of cooking food even that simple action made her feel faint. And the story Olka told, though it solved the mystery of the map, was in its way more frightening than reassuring. ''I want to see my father.'' She tried to speak clearly, spacing the words, so they would be certain to understand.

''And your father wants to see you.'' A stocky young man with a balding head and a curly reddish gold beard was speaking from the doorway. His bright blue eyes were smiling. ''The Russians have nasty drugs, so he has a headache still, but that will go away. He's foggy, too, about a lot that's happened, so for a while, I wouldn't question him too much. Otherwise, there's no reason why you can't soon be on your way."

Before he had finished speaking, Megan had darted past Győrgy, through the doorway into the adjoining room, and flung herself into her father's outstretched arms.

Muffled endearments and questions came from the region of his tweedy shoulder and the top of her head.

"You're all right?"

"*You're* all right?"

"You're *sure*?"

"*You're* sure?"

Nods, kisses and more questions followed one after the other before they took time to draw apart and look at each other. Megan saw lines of tiredness in her father's face, but she'd seen those before when he'd worked late at night or come home from one of his secret missions. Nor was she startled by the two-day growth of scratchy whiskers. Sometimes, when they were at the shack in Maine, he'd skip shaving for several days because, he said, he wanted to "rest" his face.

Only one thing was really different. And that was something she'd never seen before. Tears in her father's eyes.

There were a thousand questions Megan wanted to ask her father, but if Győrgy said they must wait until later, she would wait. In a few more hours, after the effect of the drug was largely dissipated, they could talk.

Actually, now there was scarcely time for her father to do more than shave and put on a clean shirt, and for Megan to wash her hands and face and do something to her hair before leaving for the airport where András had managed to make reservations for their direct flight, via BEA, to Helsinki. It left within the hour.

Megan was misty-eyed as she said good-bye to Olka and, because she had nothing else, gave her the little gold anchor pin that held the red tie on her sailor dress.

Olka's eyes, too, were bright with unshed tears as she took it and hugged Megan, whispering, "Come back to Budapest someday. Come back when Hungary is free."

Gÿorgy gave her a hearty, bone-crunching handshake. "Tell America 'hello.' Someday, we will elect our leaders as you do. When they are good, we keep them. When they are bad, we throw them out." His laugh was infectious. "It is good for the people to be boss."

Emotion was welling up in her, drowning anything sensible she might have said. "Thank you for letting us use your car."

Gÿorgy looked pleased. "Someday, perhaps, I can put new motors in people like I put them in that old car."

András, who had gone out to the car with Megan's father, was looking at his watch as he came in through the back door. "We'd better get started. I don't want you hanging around out there at the airport a minute longer than necessary, but neither do I want you to miss that plane."

Gÿorgy looked troubled. "You're sure you don't want me to drive them out? What if Dozsás should see you? After all, aren't you supposed to be in Székesfehérvár?"

143

"Well, yes. But I don't think either Dozsás or his friend Boris will be there. They had their chance to get the information they wanted from Megan's father and they muffed it. I don't think they're going to try again at the airport, and in broad daylight."

"In any case, old friend," said Gÿorgy softly, "be careful. For Hungary. You know there aren't too many of us around."

András pulled the car into a short-time parking space at the end of a long line of little taxicabs like the one they had ridden in the night she arrived in Budapest. "Gÿorgy's right," he said. "Although I don't see any signs of Dozsás' Mercedes, I think it might be better if I didn't go in with you. I'll try to get a porter to help with your bags."

"*I'll* get a porter." It was her father speaking from the back seat. "It will do me good to stretch my legs." Before András could remonstrate, Thomas More had eased his length out of the car and smiled his slow, easy smile. "It will also serve the purpose of giving you two a chance to say 'good-bye.' "

How smart her father was, Megan thought. So perceptive and so clever. But saying *good-bye* to András had a final, fatal sound.

András was holding her hand, stroking her fingers as he had done when they'd looked at the view from the hills of Buda.

"Maybe we don't really have to say 'good-bye,' " Megan said in a small strained voice. "Maybe you could come to the United States and go to school. Study butterflies . . . anything you want. My father and mother would help you.''

"I know. Your father spoke to me about it when I went out to the car with him at Gÿorgy's. His offer was generous . . . very kind . . .''

Megan's heart lilted. "Then, why don't you come? Oh, András, please. We would have such fun . . . such good times, and then you needn't worry about Dr. Dozsás ever again. Then, maybe someday . . .'' She paused, first in alarm, and then laughed. Happiness had made her brazen! She was proposing to a boy and didn't care!

András had put down her hand as if the action would sever the connection that bound them. "Love . . . love of one's country . . . it's impossible to explain. But I must stay here. Work for her . . . work with people like Gÿorgy, Olka and all my other friends as long as I am useful.''

From fifty feet away, Megan saw her father coming, trailed by a porter with a luggage cart.

"But we can write,'' she said. "If I knew where to write you. Or, you could write me.''

"It would not be safe, at least for a while.''

"How will I know?''

"I don't know, but I'll find a way. I'm sure to find a way if you will let me . . . kiss you again.''

"Some music is what is needed,'' said the porter. He gave Megan and András an approving look, then delicately turned away. "Had I known I would see this happy sight so early in the morning, I would have brought to work with me my violin. Something by Bartók would be very nice.''

Her father had paused several feet away and was intently studying a vapor trail slicing the early morning sky.

Megan got out of the car but did not turn around as András drove away. Back straight, head held high, she followed her father and the grinning porter into the airport.

Inside, all went smoothly. So smoothly, in fact, that had the idea not been so completely preposterous, Megan would have thought that someone was actually speeding their departure. The expenditure vouchers she and her father had been required to exchange for *forints* were accepted without questions being asked. A pleasant, uniformed woman took their passports and, after removing their Hungarian visas, returned them with a polite "Come see us again someday." A superficial examination was made of her little blue suitcase but neither her father's bag nor his briefcase was opened.

Throughout it all, Megan eyed her father anxiously. Although he was holding himself erect and speaking almost normally, she could tell it took enormous effort to do so. His face, which in the dark little parlor at Gÿorgy's house had looked merely tired, in the clear light of morning looked almost haggard.

In another fifteen minutes they could board their plane. In another fifteen minutes or so after that, they would be airborne. But not until then would the numbing apprehension about her father's health and their safe return to the free world begin to diminish. Not until then would the anaesthetizing quality of fear wear away and the pain of knowing that she would never see András again take its place.

When her father said quietly, "It's Dozsás," seconds passed before the message registered and she raised her eyes to see the familiar rotund figure coming toward them.

The fat man was beaming. "Such an early hour for departing Budapest! Still, I felt that it was only proper that I should come to wish you—what shall I say, Bon Voyage? I dare say that marine expression will have to do until someone thinks of a suitable phrase for departing airplane travelers."

When her father turned around and walked a short distance away, Dr. Dozsás looked after him, clucking a little, then addressed himself to Megan. "For him, a proud man, I know it has not been easy. But you, my dear, are the foolish one. So unnecessary and so dangerous that you should have indulged in the foolish rescue of your father *after* he had given away the secret."

"He didn't!" Megan cried. "He couldn't!"

"Oh, yes. It is true. You have—what is your American phrase—you have locked the barn door after the horse has been stolen. And young András! Thinking that he is unobserved! Oh, it really is amusing! The poor lovesick lad, thinking that *we* think he is in Székesfehérvár when, of course, we know what he is doing every minute! Last night, had you stopped instead of executing that stupid maneuver by the roadside in an attempt to mislead us, we could have told you the developments."

"Developments?" Megan's voice was scratchy.

"Oh, yes, indeed. We would have told you that late yesterday afternoon your father gave us the formula so much desired by Russia for the keeping of peace in the world. After consultation with our scientists who marveled at its brilliance, we went to the castle to inform your father of his release only to find, alas, he was not there."

"I don't believe my father told you anything. I don't believe anything you tell me." Megan spoke faintly and without conviction. Since Dr. Dozsás had started his recital, her father had stood, shoulders hunched and as unmoving as if he had been carved from stone.

Dr. Dozsás shook his head. "You did not believe me when I said that each man has his price. Or should I say, priorities. For your father to change his mind, it took just one glimpse of this."

From nowhere a ring had appeared between Dr. Dozsás' plump thumb and forefinger. His small piggy eyes twinkled as he slowly turned it this way and that until the small stone took on all the colors of the rainbow.

"Such a pretty little opal." Almost negligently he dropped it into Megan's hand. "A pity, is it not, that for you it was unlucky?"

Epilogue

MEGAN WAS SITTING with Kate in the Cades' big bay window looking out over the lovely greenness of Green Park. They were eating apples. Kate took a large, crunchy bite, reducing the apple only slightly, and said, "Now start at the beginning and tell me everything."

It was the opportunity Megan had been waiting for ever since she had arrived in London from Helsinki only an hour before. Kate was also an appreciative audience as Megan had known she would be—squealing and holding her breath in all the right places. Her eyes grew misty as Megan described her farewell to András, and she clapped her hands over her mouth to stifle a scream when told about Dr. Dozsás' appearance at the airport and what had happened afterward.

"How awful!" she breathed, looking down at Megan's opal ring winking in the sunshine. "How awful, after all you and András went through to rescue your father, only to discover that you were too late—that he'd already *told*. And how awful for *him*. I mean, how un-man-for-all-seasonish for someone named Thomas More.''

"Not really," Megan said. "You don't know everything yet. After the plane was in the air, my father told me about Dr. Dozsás and Boris kidnapping him outside the hotel and taking him to the dungeon of the palace of the Hungarian kings. There—when they found they couldn't pry a single thing out of him—Dr. Dozsás tried using my opal ring for blackmail. Fortunately, by then my father had figured out a way to tell them just enough of what they wanted to know so they would think he'd told them *all* . . ." Megan's voice trailed off as she moved closer to the window.

"You mean he left out the most important part?"

"Exactly."

Kate clapped her hands. "I should have known your father would think of something clever. And who knows? Maybe you'll see András again after all! Didn't Gÿorgy say that if Dr. Dozsás found out about his working for the underground his usefulness would be ended? It might not even be safe for him to stay in Hungary now."

As she finished speaking, Kate rose to her knees and, like a bird dog at point, stared out the window. "Look! Megan, look! Isn't that András now—standing on the otherside of the street looking longingly this way? Oh, it is! It's András! It's him!"

"I know," said Megan happily. She had, indeed, been watching him for some little time. Her eyes were very keen.

About The Author

JEANNETTE EYERLY was graduated from the State University of Iowa with a degree in English and journalism, has taught creative writing, and has contributed to major national magazines.

Mrs. Eyerly has established a reputation as a writer who tackles the delicate situations and difficult problems faced by today's teen-agers. She is a pioneer in exploring such subjects as unwed motherhood, school drop-outs, mental illness, the problems confronting children of divorced or alcoholic parents, and the conflicts of a young girl seeking a legal abortion.